Zaf straightened to his full height. He towered over her, but somehow it hadn't mattered before. "I want you to let me do my job."

The man was prince of the cloak-and-dagger. "Which is what?"

"Protecting you."

Joey halted, taking a moment to seek out the lie in his face, but she couldn't break through. She saw a man she'd missed even as she cursed the sweltering summer day she'd met him seven years ago. All she could seem to attach herself to were the memories of lazy conversations and how he altruistically volunteered his life for the law. Lean and carelessly sexy with that serious, brooding look that magnetized people even as it pushed them away, he was the Zaf her heart recognized.

But the guy who'd manipulated her into a confrontation? That screamed Archangel. It was his modus operandi.

"Goodbye, Zaf." She skirted around him to the other side of the handrail.

"Wait, please," he said, matching her steps but keeping the rail between them. "You can't look me square in the eye and say you haven't wondered if somebody's tailing you."

"Yes, I've wondered." She'd also wondered if paranoia was making her crazy. "Now I know I was right, and the doer is you."

Dear Reader,

So we've reached the end. I say goodbye to a cast of complicated and fascinating strangers who allowed me to create their glamorous, gritty world with all the sincerity and energy my heart can hold.

One More Night with You is the final book in the Blue Dynasty series. Josephine de la Peña has been waiting perched on the sidelines as everyone around her found their happily-ever-afters. It was my duty to give her something she doesn't quite believe in: a happy ending of her own. She and her hero, Zaf Ahmadi, break the mold of my books on a multitude of levels. They demanded nothing less than an explosively powerful and sexy conclusion. This story is my gift to them, and it's a bittersweet farewell to characters who've become as real to me as friends.

Thank you, dear readers, for taking the journey with me.

XOXO,

Lisa Marie Perry

One
MORE NIGHT
WITH *You*

Lisa Marie Perry

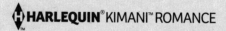

HARLEQUIN® KIMANI™ ROMANCE

Recycling programs
for this product may
not exist in your area.

ISBN-13: 978-0-373-86443-0

One More Night with You

Copyright © 2016 by Lisa Marie Perry

Printed in U.S.A.

Lisa Marie Perry encounters difficult fictional men and women on a daily basis. She writes contemporary romance fiction with plenty of sizzle, energy and depth. Flawed, problematic, damaged characters are welcome. Her tales feature sexy guy-next-door heroes and powerful larger-than-life alphas who are brought to their knees by the love of complicated women. She has received high praise from *USA TODAY* and has been nominated for an *RT Book Reviews* literary award. She lives in America's heartland, and she has every intention of making the Colorado mountains her new stomping grounds. She drives a truck, enjoys indie rock, collects Medieval literature, watches too many comedies, has a not-so-secret love for lace and adores rugged men with a little bit of nerd.

Books by Lisa Marie Perry

Harlequin Kimani Romance

Visit the Author Profile page at Harlequin.com for more titles.

For Charlotte, Danica, Martha, Bindi & Joey—

Each of you helped me become a better writer
and a more open-minded person.
Let's have a drink to that, shall we?

Chapter 1

When it came to staging an ambush, the Blues were experts.

A husband and wife, united in every power play and business venture, they controlled elite society as effortlessly as a champion manipulated a novice in games of risk and didn't respond well to the word *no*.

Josephine de la Peña had considered herself doubly exempt from their exploitation—she was a retired DEA field agent *and* their daughter's best friend. She had never before been their target. But she knew what they were capable of and this setup, schemed and executed to perfection, had their prints all over it.

Mierda!

Wrapped in a fitted pantsuit that had been sexy but wilted in a graceless surrender to wrinkles and sweat and coffee stains, accessorized with waning makeup and a pissed-off sneer, she could loiter at the entrance to the Palazzo's CUT steak house only so long before her presence summoned a tempest of unwanted attention. The curiosity in the hostess's demeanor had already darkened to suspicion because her sociable, "Would you like to be seated?" remained unanswered. And Joey, trapped in a rush of hot indignation, was flustered. Caught unawares. Totally off her game.

It might be possible to counterattack and beat the Blues at their own wheeler-dealing. Was it even too late to turn and run? Or hobble, because her walking stick wasn't a magician's wand and could do only so much for her permanent limp.

Marshall and Temperance had apparently recruited her supervisor to lay on the pressure, and the three of them sat in the exquisite ritzy glory of Joey's favorite steak house sharing a round of drinks. Scotch, if her boss had his way.

A toast to the idiot, she thought, her mind whirring, blazing, as she imagined them raising their shot glasses in anticipation of cornering her. Blame them, she would— and did, vehemently. But she'd flown into the jar and let them twist on the lid. She could be at home stripping off her clothes and the workday if she hadn't ignored her instincts. Since putting down stakes in this city, she'd become too soft, trusting, weak to manipulation. Perhaps it was a blessing that she was an inactive DEA agent, off field assignments, a Department of Justice researcher confined to a desk. No more than a civilian with a few valuable contacts and a firearm.

If she'd resisted her gut reaction to leap at the chance to eat a steak, if she'd at least had the sense to think past her celebrity crush on Wolfgang Puck, then she would've seen this dinner invitation for the ploy it was.

For one thing, her supe never singled out a team member. Whether someone screwed up or succeeded, the entire Las Vegas Office of Diversion Control knew about it.

For another, the Blues had responded uncharacteristically kindly when she'd flat-out denied the favor they'd asked of her. Divide her time between ODC and a roster of NFL players suspected of illegal drug use? She wouldn't do it.

Couldn't.

Logistically, it was virtually impossible. She was damaged, physically unqualified to babysit muscle-bound athletes and split open their secrets. What did they expect her to do, anyway? Go all Bad Cop and use her stick to whack confessions out of their men?

She didn't exactly know what they expected because she hadn't given them the opportunity to bog her down with specifics. She didn't own the Las Vegas Slayers; the Blues did. Maintaining a healthy roster was their responsibility, not hers. And she'd do herself one hell of a favor to keep away from that particular championship-winning, scandal-tainted team.

A fear-motivated attitude, but so what? She wasn't invincible. The bullet fragments embedded in her hip made that clear. The cane in her hand reminded her every day what a solitary gunshot had taken away.

"Ma'am. If you're not dining here, would you mind...?" Lips drawn in a fake-pleasant smile, the hostess carved a hand through the air in a universal *get the hell out of the way* gesture. "We need to keep this area clear for customers."

As if a five-three, one-hundred-twenty-pounds-soaking-wet woman was taking up too much space. Beside her, a group of folks thumbing smartphones and spewing conversation lazily assembled. Escaping now would be pathetically easy—just blend into the fray then slip out of the restaurant and disappear in the tide of luxury chasers pursuing The Shoppes at the Palazzo.

Except she wasn't a coward. And someone owed her a damn steak.

"I'm staying. Straight ahead there, passing around what's probably one of your most expensive bottles of liquor?" Allowing the hostess a moment to sling her critical gaze from Joey's hair—which the triple-digit summer heat was relentlessly bending to its will—to the party in question, she cleared her throat. "Yeah. They're expecting me."

"*They* are?" The woman faltered when Marshall Blue crooked two fingers at Joey. "So they are. I'll escort you, and can I have a server bring you a drink? A chilled cocktail, perhaps?"

A seat in front of the wine wall and a fat slice of caramelized banana cream pie wouldn't be so bad, but there was business to be done here. "Thanks, but I've got this."

The pressure, the slick setups, they ended here—tonight. She should be more offended than she was, but she held her supervisor in the highest regard and loved the Blues as her own.

Grip tight on the walking stick, Joey did her best to barrel toward the main dining room. Modern, upscale elegance dripped from the chandeliers, reflected in the windows and art, shimmered in the very ambience of the place. She caught the teeny pops of cell phone camera flashes as people photographed their entrées, and almost smiled despite how irked she was at the three people standing to greet her.

"No private table?"

"Waitstaff, photographers, they pay extra close attention to the private tables," Ozzie Salvinski answered neutrally, resuming his seat. "You're late."

Marshall snagged her hand in a hard shake that spared no consideration for her size, then let his wife lean in to buss the air beside Joey's cheeks. God forbid Temperance Blue ruin her perfect lip color application by making contact with actual skin.

"And you lied to me," Joey responded evenly. "What's

the payout for getting me here, Ozzie? Season tickets? Box seats?"

Ozzie was up again, springing off the chair like a jack-in-the-box in spite of his bulk and the usually calm, deliberate way he carried himself. Bladelike nose, grizzled jaw, muddy amber eyes—they formed an angry palette, confronting her dead-on. "You implying I can be bought? Don't do it. Don't make that mistake, damn it. I've been on the right side of the law longer than you've been alive."

But Ozzie wasn't a black-and-white, right-is-right-and-wrong-is-wrong kind of guy. She didn't exactly doubt his heart rested on the side of justice, but in the four years since she'd given up DEA gigs in DC and taken up residence at Vegas's ODC, she had observed her supervisor get a little *creative* with the rules to make things happen.

Not to mention Ozzie was a middle-class man with a minimalist blue-collar lifestyle, and Joey would wager her designer shoe collection the man wouldn't be breaking bread with a pair of billionaires if they hadn't sought him out for very exact reasons—reasons that had everything to do with coercing her to do a job for them.

"Here's what I know, then. I get an invitation for steak, which ought've tipped me off, because you've never treated me to anything more extravagant than a street vendor hot dog. Imagine my thoughts when I walk in and find you with the Blues drinking—" she braced her weight on the stick and reached across the glass table to pick up their bottle "—Scotch. Of course. What am I supposed to be thinking, boss?"

"I think," Tem intervened, dismissing Ozzie and settling a pair of unblemished brown hands on Joey's face. Without question, she found perspiration beneath her fingertips, but she didn't recoil. The need to get a point across overtook the utter ick factor of encountering someone else's sweat. "I think, Josephine, that a tantrum is neither appropriate

nor attractive for a woman your age. Ah, sure, keep frowning like that and ask yourself why you can't hold a man's
interest with your clothes on."

"Are you calling me a mattress? It's not the wisest
way to get a favor." Fact was, guys rarely held *her* interest outside of sex. If sex was the sum of her connection
with someone, she wouldn't apologize for taking what she
could.

"You're insulted." Tem looked puzzled.

"Because you *insulted* me." No one understood the complications, strings and catch-22s that came attached to Joey's
every attempt at a genuine romance. "Please don't go there."

"Well, it's the same thing I'd tell my daughters." Tem
tried to tuck a few errant curls behind Joey's ears but
quickly gave up on the effort and took her seat with a
dainty plop. She then none-too-discreetly began wiping
her hands on a napkin. "Why don't you try on a sweeter
disposition sometime? It couldn't hurt."

"Thanks, Tem, but I already have parents."

"Who are in Texas. Would you please sit down already?
Folks are beginning to stare and this—" she ran a finger up
and down to indicate Joey's sweaty, wrinkled appearance
"—likely isn't the impression you want them to take away.
Goodness knows, I wouldn't appreciate an irate woman's
outburst wrecking my dining experience."

And now *I understand just why Charlotte was talking about eloping.* The words were practically slamming
against Joey's teeth, demanding to be released, but she'd
promised her best friend she'd lock the info away in the
vault. Many months ago Charlotte had mentioned she and
her fiancé might marry in secret to sidestep their families'
Montague-Capulet drama. She'd abandoned the thought
and was now planning a very traditional, very expensive
August wedding. Still, the conflict rained fire and brim-

stone on them, and Joey regretted the minor—or not, depending on who you asked—role she played in it all.

Lowering onto a chair, propping the stick against the table, she addressed each of them with a stoic glance. "Boss," she said to Ozzie, "how about you pour me a Scotch and tell me why you tricked me into coming here."

"Tricked." He spat the word, swinging up the bottle and turning a shot glass upright on a tray. "I said meet me here for a steak. So help me, you're gonna leave here with steak in your belly."

Joey accepted the drink, turning it up without pause. Welcoming the impact of the liquid saturating her taste buds, she signaled for another. "What do they want from me, exactly?"

"Ask them."

"No." She relaxed against her chair, sank the next drink. "I'm asking you, sir."

"Somebody's using. Cocaine, marijuana, meth. The team's management put together a training camp drug prevention program. So running workshops, looking after the men, staying alert and making things look straight and narrow for the press. In the vein of the substance abuse prevention you dealt with at those schools back in the day."

Not so far back, technically. In between Fed cases, she'd touted DARE and other drug education programs to K-12 institutions and universities as part of community outreach. But it felt as though a lifetime had passed since she'd been the agent—the woman—she once was.

"Yeah, I get the basic idea. Marshall and Tem pitched it to me before. I told them no, so why don't you tell me why you can't get DEA on this?" She shut up when a server appeared at their table with menus and a bottle of Pinot Noir. The Blues let the server fill two glasses and depart with the bottle, as both Joey and Ozzie were good with Scotch for now.

"We have something specific in mind for you," Marshall said, settling his obsidian-black gaze on her. As a child she'd been taught to study faces, and this mountain of a man had one of the most interesting ones she had ever seen. She liked to think of him as comprised of stones and rocks—bald head, prominent jaw, wide shoulders—yet the ingredients of his personality could be found in the details of his facial features. The gray-touched mustache and beard framed a scowling mouth; the hard-edged eyes seemed to always expose an unprovoked threat. *Give me a reason to make you sorry you crossed me*, they implored. But the creases etched deep into his dark skin, especially the carvings between his brows and bracketing his mouth, revealed a man staggering under immense pressure...a man who worried.

A man who had taken a few brutal bumps and found out he wasn't invincible. She could relate to that. Besides, in him she saw glimpses of her own father—someone she missed daily but spoke to only a fraction as often.

"What, Marshall? It's impractical to think you can browbeat me into chasing your football players around training camp. My duties are to ODC. And there's the drive. You'd be asking me to do a Vegas–Mount Charleston commute."

"We'll compensate you for the mileage," Tem offered. "Or provide you with an entirely new vehicle."

New, for Tem, probably meant *showroom* new. Not that Joey wasn't loyal to her vintage Chevy Camaro, but a brand-new car was enticing—*and stop. Concentrate.* "Um...thank you, but no. I want to focus on the career I have and not this side narc gig. Charlotte's a trainer—does she know about this initiative?"

"Yes." Tem sipped her Pinot Noir.

"What about the part you want me to play?"

"To a degree."

Joey sighed, considering her empty shot glass. She

wouldn't fill it again until after she got some food down. "Why me, then? What is this really about? Spare me the charades and say what's up."

Ozzie raised his eyebrows at the Blues then splashed more Scotch into his glass and said nothing.

"We think of you as family," Tem began. "You're loyal, noble, intelligent—"

"Quit complimenting me. I'm not used to it." She looked from wife to husband. "What's the gig?"

Marshall leaned, spoke quietly. "To the media, you'll be just another drug prevention leader. To the Slayers, you'll be a friend. They'll want to loosen up, talk, get close."

"Oh, I get what's up." She addressed Tem. "This is why you suggest I work on a *sweeter disposition*? To get your men hot under the uniform? Why you'd court that kind of distraction on your field, I don't know."

"No one's advising you to sleep with them. Ask your friend Charlotte how our organization responds to inter-office affairs."

"Gosh. And here I was thinking the prospect of football player nookie might be a perk. Way to kill the dream."

"I'm dead serious. Sex with our players is prohibited. Should you violate this stipulation, you'll be pulled off the assignment. Ozzie can handle further disciplinary action as he sees appropriate."

"So tease them?"

"Josephine, you're being facetious," Tem accused, shifting her attention to the menu. "Were you this difficult when the feds put you on assignments? Or is this bitterness something that set in after you were shot?"

"Spare me the psychology trip, Tem. I'm ready to select my steak now."

To her relief, the others relented—at least long enough to consult the menus and order appetizers and entrées. With conversation centered on food for the moment, Joey let herself absorb the cool air and the thick aroma of gourmet offerings. Anticipating a sirloin with potatoes and paired with a burgundy, she observed the Blues. They had riches and power beyond her comprehension, yet she felt sorry for them. Because that was the thing with ultimate wealth and success—once you found it you spent an eternity struggling to defend it.

A basket of pretzel bread arrived, and Joey didn't waste a moment dissecting a piece right along with the sparse info the Blues had shared. "Persuade the players to get chatty with me. That's what you're asking, hmm?"

"That's right," Tem confirmed. "The championship win was a high in and of itself. While we expected our men to celebrate, some of them have a false sense of security and invulnerability. Staff adjustments and trades have made things hectic, but Marshall and I aren't out of touch. As Salvinski told you, someone's in deep. Take a closer look at our kicker, TreShawn Dibbs."

Joey had heard the athlete's name on sports TV and radio often enough for one league violation or another. He was a risk to any team that took him on, but the Blues had acquired that risk because the man could win games. "Is he friends with Charlotte? Why haven't you asked her to monitor things or have a heart-to-heart with him?"

"The dynamic of her friendship with him is why we're not involving her in this process. She's protective of him. Her judgment's compromised," Tem said. "Now, then. Dibbs may not be the only user, but if we need to make an example that no man is indispensable, then we will. We need the identities of the users and the suppliers."

"That kind of admission won't come from a 'Hey, how's it going?' chat."

"Precisely why it's vital that you build a rapport. Gaining trust is key. Camp starts this month, after the rookie symposium. We'll need you to stay out of the way during practice, but be near. Find out who goes where when they're off the field and go with them. Get yourself on the right guest lists. Make them believe you're kosher."

"Meaning act as if I talk the drug-free game but secretly I'm down with using?"

Tem shrugged a slim shoulder and drummed her fingers across the bejeweled neckline of her white silk crepe dress. "You'll know what measures to take when an opportunity presents itself. Just do what's necessary to collect the information we require. And do it with your clothes on."

"Had to add that, didn't you?"

Tem sighed. "All right, I apologize."

"What's your endgame? A clean roster?"

"Think of it more as cleaning the roster. The NFL has a substance abuse policy in place, which we intend to enforce. But we'd prefer to avoid PR disasters this season, so the sooner and quieter we can nip this problem in the bud, the better."

So this went beyond helping drug abusers break free of a dangerous threat that might cost them careers, families and perhaps their lives. "You want me to coax the users out of hiding just so you can cut them from the team? Do you care whether or not they get help? And suppose someone else picks them up—don't those teams deserve the courtesy of knowing what demons come with these men?"

"Our role," Marshall said, folding his massive hands on the table in front of him, "is to protect the Las Vegas Slayers franchise. We will accept nothing short of excellence. We won't have our championship pissed on by a damn addict. Do what you have to do to get the information we need, then put it in our hands. It's simple."

"Actually, no, it's not. What makes you believe it'd be simple? The team put your daughter through one hell of a rite of passage last year. I have neither the time nor the interest in experiencing that just for kicks."

The man pulled a note from his billfold, scribbled something with a heavy hand then pushed it across the table to her. Joey's mouth dropped open and a piece of pretzel bread tumbled out.

"God help us, she's an Eliza Doolittle," Tem murmured woefully, but Joey was too shaken by the figure scrawled in front of her to react to the insult.

"That kind of money isn't for a *just for kicks* job," Marshall said. "As a thank-you and a gesture of goodwill, we've arranged for a substantial donation to the city as well as the Good Samaritans of Nevada. That's the certified prevention and treatment agency assisting us. Everything is aboveboard."

"Then why would I be compensated?"

Ozzie said, "You're taking an unpaid leave of absence from ODC while you're working the Slayers job. Your income's got to come from someplace."

They'd thought of everything, as though the decision had been made but consulting her was a pesky formality.

"And if I say no?"

Marshall and Tem's expressions dimmed, and Ozzie stood. "Come with me to the bar, Joey. I want a different drink and ain't keen on drinking alone."

"So you're going to have peanuts with it?" she quipped, though she was pushing back her chair and reaching for the walking stick.

To the Blues, Ozzie asked, "Are you sure you want this one? She's got an attitude that'll raise your blood pressure. Sometimes I wonder if it's worth it."

Joining him in the lounge, Joey weakly cuffed her supervisor on the arm. "Your high blood pressure has more to do with sports super-fandom and a salt-heavy diet than it does with me, Ozzie."

"Eh, you're probably right." He signaled to the bartender

and ordered them each a custom cocktail. "But so what, Joey? Take the assignment."

"Are you eager to be rid of me for a while?"

"That's a bullshit thing to say. You're competent. More than that, to be honest. That synthetic drug case we just wrapped up—your research was brilliant. You came to us with impeccable credentials, stellar recommendations—"

"And three legs," she added, raising the stick.

"The sooner you stop thinking of it that way, the happier you'll be. Guarantee it. Until then, you need a new challenge, something away from the desk. What the Blues want you to do for them, that's a taste of what you're used to. Going undercover, breathing in all that risk and action."

"Deceiving folks," she whispered, finding his amber eyes sympathetic. Could she truly convey to anyone that a career in DEA had been both heaven and hell? "Lying about who I am. Earning trust in order to twist it into a weapon."

"It was all to serve a greater good."

The relationships she'd severed, the victims she couldn't save, the men she'd come to for sex but had hurt eventually—and the man who'd devastated her—they'd all been casualties. On the other side of that was all the destruction she'd helped prevent and the frail comfort of knowing she was true to her duty to the law and fulfilled an allegiance to a country that depended on the loyalty of its soldiers.

Years of protecting and serving America, empty days highlighted by the immeasurable sacrifices she'd made to hunt criminals, had brought her here—vulnerable and relying on a stick.

"What's the greater good in this situation?" She pushed her cocktail toward Ozzie and let him knock it back. It'd take another half dozen to jiggle loose his sobriety. The man's tipping point was legendary. "The Blues extract a couple of drug abusers from their team. Men lose their jobs and may not get the kind of aid they need to turn things around."

"Chances are the dealers are operating in wider markets. Getting illicit drugs to kids, even. So we do what we need to do to shut 'em down. But look, Joey, nobody's asking you to be a superhero. That's not what DEA's about, and not what this job with the Slayers is about."

"Then tell me, Ozzie, what's the greater good?"

"Could be there isn't a clear one," he said bluntly. "At the end of all this, though, if you can stop feeling like a victim, then it's worth it." He stood, left a few bills for the bartender and pointed to her stick. "It's a cane, Joey. That's all it is. And with the money the Blues are throwing at you, you can feed that fancy shoe fetish of yours. Get over the ego trip. Consider the opportunity."

She sat at the bar among a gathering of people she didn't know, as music beat in her ears and her thoughts competed for priority. On contract with the Slayers, she'd be wading into a high-profile world she knew only through her friendship with Charlotte.

Having a friend on the training staff might certainly help Joey become acclimated with the team. But Charlotte wouldn't know the full truth behind Joey's contract. Their friendship would be shaded with lies, shadowed under a layer of deceit.

Not ideal circumstances, but what if in the end the franchise and the Blue family could be on a real path toward recovery? What if a little bit of lying on her part could secure their chance for a fresh start in the wake of a tumultuous year?

Returning to the table, she announced, "I made a decision."

They watched her in expectant silence.

"I'm accepting the gig. And I want dessert."

Chapter 2

"You're a tough woman to pin down."

The echoing voice stabbed into the quiet gymnasium training room, throwing off Joey's hand-eye coordination and causing her uppercut to miss the punching dummy's jaw. Off balance, she stumbled forward, and her left hip started to throb.

She swore, clinging to the six-foot mannequin's shoulders, and grinded her teeth against the pain. "*Ay, Dios mio!* Lottie, I'm stressed, carb-deprived and jonesing to hit something. *I* wouldn't want to be near me right now."

The twenty-four-hour Main Street gym was the watering hole where a number of Joey's colleagues gathered to sweat off calories and exchange gossip. Today she was alone, taking advantage of a predawn workout. Last night at CUT she'd practically binged, and she'd skipped her first-thing-in-the-morning stretches, which explained her pelvic stiffness.

"Answer me this." Charlotte Blue, wearing a cream-colored jumper and a floral herbal fragrance, sauntered forward to stand behind the dummy and peek over its shoulder. "Is this the closest you've been to a man since Parker?"

"If you intend to go on about him, you can turn around and get the hell out of here. I mean that."

Parker Brandt, an LVMPD officer with a cute kid and a grin that made her forget herself, was supposed to be a summer fling but she'd lost control of the relationship. At a crossroads, trying to figure out whether or not what they had might be love, they'd ended up taking off in different directions.

Parker had cut into her orbit again several weeks ago. The sex had been rough with desperation neither of them wanted to acknowledge, but it was a superficial thrill, satisfaction so fragile that she'd left his bed in an emotional fog. She could no longer mourn the relationship; could no longer force herself to miss him. It was closure, yet it left her at loose ends.

She had circled back to that strange place she found herself each time she ended things with a lover, harping on the past again, stuck in old dreams of the treachery and violence and heartbreak that had stolen her capacity to move on. It'd been practically five years since the shooting, but it might as well have been five minutes.

She would never be free.

"I need to dig into this workout, all right?" She'd been at it over two hours already, stirring around endorphins, trying to burn off tension, but what did trivial details matter? "Whatever you tracked me down for, let's talk about it later."

Concern pulled at Charlotte's full lips. "If the guy's name can incite rage, then you need to put some things in check."

"It's not that." Balancing her weight to her uninjured

hip, she mopped her face with the bottom of her midriff top. It wasn't about Parker, who'd been a diversion to keep her body sated. In DEA, *diversions* and one-time-only sex had been practical. After she'd packed her stuff in her Camaro and driven toward a new life in Nevada, they'd become few and far between. "We weren't aiming for an engagement and a happily-ever-after."

"But Parker thought you were, didn't he?"

"He was mistaken. That's meant for some people, like you and your fiancé. But as for me—" she shrugged, gave her best attempt at a carefree laugh "—I'm meant for something else. Good times. Flings. One-nighters."

Charlotte smiled, hooking her arm around the mannequin's neck. A mane of curly ebony coils bobbed about her shoulders. "Then let discretion be your friend. My parents might not react too kindly to paparazzi catching you taking walks of shame. It won't reflect so well on the franchise, is what they'd say."

"Spoken from experience? Who caught you sneaking out of Nate Franco's place with your panties in your hand?" About this time last year Charlotte had struck up a naughty affair with a fellow trainer—who also happened to be the son of the team's shady previous owner. A suspension, a resignation and a hell of a lot of drama had ensued, but Joey tried not to linger on that.

Where her moral compass had guided her, and what she'd done in the name of friendship and for the sake of the law, still weighed on her. Somewhere in the recesses of her thoughts was a sense of dread that whispered her day of reckoning awaited her.

Maybe the unexplainable feeling that she was being followed wasn't so crazy, after all. But she wouldn't tell Charlotte that.

"I'm Marshall and Temperance Blue's employee first

and their daughter second," Charlotte said. "What's best for the business prevails over all else."

"That is effing depressing."

"A fact that's not likely to change, and what you can look forward to, now that you've joined the drug prevention initiative. But I predict Ma and Pop will be spending more time at the stadium than at camp. Let's hope that gives you some breathing room."

"They told you I said yes?"

"Ma did. Last night we met up with the seamstress for another gown fitting. More alterations to be done. Oh, hang on, I need to download some veil designs." She plucked her phone from an embossed leather handbag. A couple of taps and swipes and she dropped the phone back inside. "So the reason I found you this morning is about the wedding. You never confirmed that you'd be my maid of honor."

Right, *that*. Charlotte had asked last month and Joey was still stalling. Rejecting the honor would hurt her friend's feelings. But accepting when all she could imagine was limping down the aisle and enduring the reception without a date to keep her company didn't seem fair, either. So she'd held off, finding reasons to avoid the conversation.

"The wedding is next month. Nate and I need to know."

"Have you asked your sisters or any of your other friends?"

"No. I asked you. I chose you."

"But I can't, Lottie."

"Why not?"

"Can you not let this go? Are you that much like your parents?"

"The Blues usually don't give up pursuit without a good fight. I didn't come here to fight with you, though. I'm here to tell you that you're my friend and I want you to be maid of honor." She averted her eyes then edged away from the punching dummy. "Are you hesitating because of Nate? Do you not approve?"

"We tabled this issue, didn't we? Nate's fine."

"His family's not. His father attempted suicide a few months ago. And his godfather—" The interior doors to the gymnasium were hauled open and a cluster of people in sweats fiddling with MP3 players, phones and activity trackers trooped inside. "You know where I'm going with this."

And his godfather was arrested. But Gian DiGorgio was a free man again, having been released a few short weeks after being collected in a police cruiser. Joey had followed the developments through federal contacts who knew what was happening before the media could sense it. The man's high-roller haven casino was up for sale, a technicality had spared him an indictment on illegal gambling dealings and charges involving his attempt to procure a murder had been vacated.

Technicality be damned. The charges should have held up. They were legit, and Joey knew because she had been the one to uncover the unregulated ring Nate Franco's godfather and father were running out of the DiGorgio Royal Casino.

She'd *needed* those charges to stick. It was more than a matter of gratifying her ego or proving that her investigative skills were top-notch. DiGorgio's name was a chill skittering down her spine.

"I know exactly where you're going with this, Lottie, and I wish you wouldn't. Nate's a good man and he loves you. I pray to Mary that your marriage is a blessed one."

"But you don't want to be a part of the wedding."

Joey rested her hands against the mannequin's pectorals, leaning on it for support. "I can't."

"You won't," Charlotte corrected. Her voice was free

of accusation, gentle with compassion. "There's a difference, Jo."

"That's fair. I *won't* do it. I won't embarrass you with a cane that'll ruin the outfit."

"You look badass with the cane."

"Looking badass all the time gets tiring. Besides, I have a limp and…and…"

"And what?"

"And I'll have no date. Men don't want me because of this cane and because of this limp. When anyone looks past the damage and sees me, I tell myself 'Oh, Josephine, you'd better not be choosy. Hang on tight 'cause another man might not come around.' This is my world, Lottie. Welcome." Frustrated, Joey pushed against the dummy, landed her uppercut crisply against its jaw. Then came another punch paired with an angry, guttural scream. "Son of a bitch," she sobbed, staggering back a few steps until she wound up square on her ass on the gymnasium floor. "Son of a *bitch*!"

"Is she going to be okay?" Joey heard someone ask as she drew up her healthy leg and hugged her knee. Through a tangle of light brown strands she saw a gym employee hovering, his laminated ID badge swinging from a lanyard.

"She will. Thanks for checking up," Charlotte answered, kneeling down. "Okay, Jo, what time do you clock in today?"

"Nine sharp." *Don't ask why—just send her on her way.* "Why?"

"That gives us plenty of time. Get up, hit the shower and do something with you hair. Meet me in the lobby in thirty."

"The question bears repeating. *Why?*"

"I'm scheduling you for a sit-down with Willa Smart."

"Willa Smart is…?"

"The founder and CEO of the hottest dating company

in the West. Wait, have you never heard of Dating Done Smart? It's headquartered here in Las Vegas."

Joey released her knee and slapped her hands on the floor, blinking tears from her eyelashes. "No friggin' way. You're booking me an appointment with a *matchmaker*?"

"Willa and Ma float in the same social ponds. Her daughter and my sister are friends. Best friends, actually. Are you following along?"

"Not really, but go on."

"Anyway," Charlotte continued, straightening then holding out her hands to help Joey up, "Willa's company is award-winning. It uses this highly intelligent computerized matching system. It's all very scientific with complicated algorithms, but the approach is said to be individualized and personal. And it's confidential. No one will know unless you want them to."

"If it's so top-notch, why didn't matchmaking mama extraordinaire Tem send you and your sisters to Miz Willa?"

"None of us would allow it. She's convinced we're screwing inappropriate men just to grate her nerves. But once she found out about the engagement and I finally let Nate put a ring on my finger, she eased up on the bitching and moaning. I can be thankful for that, right?"

"I'd call that a victory." And she praised the saints that Anita Esposito de la Peña had become a non-interfering, *laissez-faire* parent once the family had made it through Joey's Quinceañera. "So. Know anyone who's used Dating Done Smart?"

"Uh-uh. At least, not personally. Word is the success rate's phenomenal. Heralded in business and lifestyle magazines. Featured in psychology journals. All that good stuff. It was mentioned during the Emmy Awards. The host made a crack about soliciting professional help to get some actress a Prince Charming."

"I'm not in the market for a Prince Charming, remember? I'm not chasing happily-ever-after. All I want is intelligent conversation and some sweaty sex. Not saying the intelligent conversation should necessarily occur *during* the sweaty sex."

"Let's try not to lead with that. But your choice." Charlotte tugged Joey upright then handed her the walking stick. "No one's saying this has to end in an 'I do' of your own. Take the compatibility test and see if it matches you to any decent talent. If things go south and you'd rather not be maid of honor, then I'll respect that and won't ask you to reconsider. Will you give it a try?"

Nope. Nope, nope, nope, nope. But she heard herself say, "*Sí*, okay."

"That was invasive."

Willa Smart's office wasn't quiet. It was alive with an orchestral melody twirling out of the room and the bleed-through of footsteps and good-morning greetings from the other side of the frosted glass doors.

Latching on to the comment, Willa sat on a white leather chair instead of releasing Joey into the wild of singles roaming the egg-frying-hot Vegas streets.

"Invasive?" The woman's finely arched brows rose and fell over eyes as dark as the Texas soil Joey missed from her childhood. "How so?"

"Completing that questionnaire was reminiscent of the LSATs."

"You took the LSATs?"

"Yeah." She'd passed, even by her severe expectations. And straightaway she'd put the exam—and Papá's wishes for her future—on the back burner. "I'm just saying, the screening process is heavy. The last time I was probed so closely, my feet were in stirrups and a speculum was involved."

Willa's expression froze. Gray, kinky hair twisted

high exposed a curiously lovely face. Freckle-dotted, fawn-colored skin. Asymmetrical cheeks. A mouth that drooped slightly on the right. "A specu— Ah, never mind. We prefer to think of our screening process as thorough, but you've found it intrusive."

"Well, yes, I guess."

"Was it overly time-consuming?"

"Just too…in-depth." In-depth, exactly. The questions held up far too many mirrors, shone light on things Joey preferred to stay in the dark. "I'm surprised no one's popped in to ask me for a pee sample."

"Your humor protects you, doesn't it?"

Her guard slipped, and the honesty was as welcoming as the touch of a cool cloth on fevered skin. "I'd like it to."

"Oh? Why?"

"If I answer that question, what will the next one be?"

"Why do you need protection?"

Joey was here as a client, not a patient. She answered Willa's scrutiny with, "Ohhh, no, you don't, Miz Willa."

"First, I quite like that—*Miz Willa*. Second, what is it that you're taking offense to now?"

"Charlotte didn't talk me into a therapy session. I'm here to meet somebody. An okay guy who can get me through my friend's wedding, help me bust a few Os along the way and back off when it's time."

"So you've assigned an expiration date to a relationship that hasn't yet formed."

Again with the psychological detour. Was this Willa Smart the matchmaker, or Willa Smart the shrink?

The decor said she'd entered a trap of the latter. Aside from being overrun with flowers, it contradicted Joey's imaginings. Behind Willa's desk was a wall of frames that showed off credentials: doctoral degrees, therapist licenses, Association for Psychological Science awards. An ultra-comfy sofa cluttered with a pile of random throw pillows prevented the space from being labeled sterile. In place of candlelight and sultry R&B music were sunshine and opera. Where she thought she might find snapshots of smiling, happily matched couples were strange photographs of barren landscapes.

Instead of shag carpeting, Joey found hardwood beneath her patent leather Christian Louboutin beauties as she paced the width of Willa's desk. "Stop, all right? I'm not dumb."

"Agreed," Willa said emphatically, consulting her tablet. "You're a crack shot. You've incapacitated attackers twice your size without the benefit of a weapon. You can solve a Rubik's cube with your breath held."

"I'm sorry, I thought my questionnaire answers were privileged info."

"And they are. You shared these facts on your welcome survey."

"Oh." A shrug. "About the Rubik's cube. That's more of a party trick. Gets a few laughs. My personal best is under three minutes, but I'm not trying to break world records."

"It still speaks to remarkable cleverness. Also damn impressive bravado."

"Point is?"

"Those answers were in response to 'What do you value most about yourself?'"

"Okay, so? I answered on a whim. Didn't realize I'd be judged on it."

"I'm not judging—"

Joey cut her off. "You are. Looking at me now and skimming a welcome survey, you think you have a handle on me. You see somebody dysfunctional, somebody unmatchable."

"Those are neither my words nor my thoughts, Josephine. Take a seat, please."

"I have to go to work—" she jerked up her wrist for a glance at her watch. 8:06 "—within the hour."

"Then I'll be brief." Willa gestured to the sofa, and when Joey sank onto the cushions and pillows she scooted her chair away from the desk and moved it directly in front of her skittish client.

"Why ditch the desk?" Joey asked.

"The desk gives the impression that I hold a position of power over whomever's on the other side. I hold no power over you, Josephine. You're free to leave at any time, but I hope you'll allow me to say my piece."

Joey rested the cane across her lap then absentmindedly laid a throw pillow on top of it. "Go ahead."

"Is that a habit, concealing your stick?"

"Willa, I underwent psychiatric evals after the shooting. I'm sure you're aware that's standard protocol for folks in law enforcement. I don't need a touch-up."

The woman conceded with a nod. "The Blues are my friends and since you're rather important to them, I feel it's my duty to impart some wisdom here. It's highly unlikely that you're unmatchable. But you're searching for something even you aren't sure you really want, as though some part of your past is unresolved."

"Trust me, short-term is what I want. I'm independent—set in my ways, as Papá would call it. I have a house, a demanding job with long hours."

"What about relationships?"

"Commitment's too restrictive for me. I have a pretty good thing going. Completely free to share my body."

"And your heart?"

"That's not up for grabs anymore. I don't feel safe anymore."

Willa watched her steadily, and as the years began to roll back to a night in a parking garage—violence that hadn't taken Joey's life but had killed some part of her all the same—the room started to close in.

Get out. Now. Blurting some excuse, she jostled the pillows aside and got to her feet. "Going forward, Willa, streamline this for me, okay? No itty-bitty steps, no internet courtship. Just get me in contact with the guy and I'll face-to-face him."

"Are you certain you'd feel safe?"

Not entirely. But she had to take control of some aspect of her life. If not this, then what? If not now, then when?

"Just set it up, Miz Willa. I can handle my life from here."

"Well, this is anticlimactic." As challenging as it was to continue up the steps to the Clark County Library—instead of surrendering to her gut's plea to bail on the stranger Dating Done Smart had dredged up for her—Joey couldn't keep the complaint sealed between her glossy Naughty Nude lips. Leaving now was an option, but one she wouldn't take. Since she hadn't parked the Camaro on Flamingo Road, she was far from escape and closer to the fate she'd agreed to days ago when notification came that she apparently wasn't undateable. Plus, risk-lust compelled her to at least get a look at him. She owed herself that.

But as far as blind dates went, this one was already off to a lackluster start. The man had suggested a library, of all venues. Not that she didn't appreciate such a place—because, hello, a building full of books!—or that she wanted a cliché meal-and-a-movie kind of afternoon. It felt too intimate...and strangely familiar, which was entirely illogical.

She'd attempted a blind date only once before, at age twelve. Considering how hellishly *that* experience had played out, it was sort of astonishing that she rallied enough courage to try it again now. So careless she'd been to sneak off her family's ranch and take a bus from El Paso to Corpus Christi to sing with a local country-star wannabe her friend Honey Sutherland had met while on a 4H Club field trip. So silly she'd been to have stars in her eyes and grown-up dreams of French kisses and music-making with some guy she didn't know, all because Honey had said he was awfully cute and drove a truck and smelled like Starburst candy. So lucky she'd been to find her parents waiting to intercept her at a depot. They'd busted up her plans and probably saved her ass.

There was no one to intercept her this time. But she was no longer careless or silly. Any naïveté or innocence she'd once had was gone. She didn't sing anymore, had forgotten the smell of Starburst and had been French-kissed in places that would disgust her twelve-year-old self.

"Say something, miss?"

Midway up the steps leading to the library's entrance, Joey paused and glanced at the hunched-shouldered man sitting with his corduroy-clad legs sprawled wide and his face cracking under a layer of sunburnt skin. "Thinking out loud. Didn't mean to disturb you."

"Aw, ha! You didn't." He jerked a skinny thumb, the nail ringed in filthy debris, toward the building behind him. "The folks coming out of there, with their damn phones and music whatchamacallits—*they* disturb me."

As he rifled through a knapsack and yanked out a hardcover and a bag of potato chips, she began to move past him.

"Can I ask you a rude question?" the man called out. Again she paused. "See, people get a look at me, expect that I've got no use for manners and all that. Or they suppose I want money from 'em."

"I don't think you want money. If you did you would've asked already."

His grin revealed a set of stained teeth, but it was sincere and perhaps the most pleasant sight she'd find on this overcast day. "The cane…"

As if she hadn't heard variations of *this* before. *What's a good-looking thing like you doing with a cane? What's wrong with you? What turned you into a cripple?*

They were words, only words, yet hauntingly painful.

"What's that made out of," he asked, "marble?"

Joey smiled, nodding. Of the four she owned, the dove-white swirl one was the least offensive to her navy pinup dress. The 1940s-era-inspired dress, with its crisp collar, short sleeves and full skirt, might've been modest if not for the plunging neckline. "Yes, it's marble. That wasn't a rude question, but I've got one of my own. What are you reading?"

"Have a look for yourself."

Peeking at her watch, discreetly assessing her surroundings and memorizing his physical details, she settled on the step beside him. The air was barely a whisper, and a stale, musty odor stung her nostrils. She reached for the book. "A biography on Copernicus. How are you finding it?"

"Pompous. I'd've made a bigger dent in it if it'd been written in plain English." A moment of hesitation preceded, "My God, there's nothing more fascinating than a pretty lady reading."

She smirked, thumbing the pages. "So is this a hobby, hanging out in front of libraries and stirring up conversations with pretty ladies?"

"Nope, miss, can't say it is. Most days I don't say much. Las Vegas is a busy place, and time's so precious that nobody seems to want to share it with folks who can't do nothing for 'em."

And how true that was, she thought, closing the book. She was here only because she thought a professional Cupid had unearthed someone who would scratch an itch so deep and intangible even she couldn't pinpoint it.

"Miss? What's ailing you?"

Scoffing, she handed him the biography. "That famously infamous question. I was shot some years ago, had a couple of surgeries and now I have a permanent walking buddy."

"Bottom of my heart, I'm sorry to know that," he said, wrinkling his brow over jaundiced eyes. "I was meaning to ask what's got you wound tighter than a two-dollar watch, but I guess that's as good an answer as any."

"Oh. Guess it is." She for sure wasn't going to ramble on about a blind date to a man who might not have a fresh change of clothes or a real bed. "Give me a potato chip, *por favor*? I'll pay you for it."

He frowned, confused, but opened the bag and shook out a few into a grimy hand. The unsanitary transaction made the food inedible, but she fished cash from her crossbody pocketbook and took the chips, anyway.

When he noticed Benjamin Franklin's face on the bill, he gasped. "Oh—no, miss—"

"Keep it," she insisted, getting up. "Take care."

"You, too, my friend."

The library appeared busier than she'd seen it on a Saturday afternoon. Joey entered the building, and gratefulness for the air-conditioning outweighed the strands of angst that were as sticky as the loose curls clinging to the nape of her neck. Born in Mexico and bred in Texas, she was accustomed to warmer temps, but this summer's humidity seemed to amplify everything—the sizzle of the sun, the heat in the atmosphere, her anxiety.

Without a makeup arsenal, her best attempt at freshening up was to wash her hands and adjust the silver heirloom combs that held her hair from her face.

A frowning face. She worked her jaw to wiggle loose some of the tension, tried on a smile but it felt too artificial. Giving up, she backed away from the restroom mirror and made her way to the lobby art gallery.

Patrons and staff zigzagged across the floor, crowded the lobby. By force of habit Joey logged the faces, stored every unique feature in her memory bank. None of them triggered suspicion, but a dull sense of apprehension built as she neared her destination—as though the spirit of someone as intimate as a lover and as dangerous as an enemy had draped an arm over her shoulders.

At the gallery she stopped short, recognizing a nosy, stubborn, ebony-haired friend. "Charlotte, what the hell?" She hadn't meant to growl, but stress had been all but choking her. "I told you I could do this without backup."

The woman had the actual nerve to look befuddled as she turned around. "Sometimes I forget how talented you are at putting the *ass* in *assumption*. Who says I'm not here to get at look at CCL's collections?"

"Are you?"

"All right, no, I'm not. I came to watch out for you." Charlotte, in leggings and a Las Vegas Slayers polo shirt, had clearly driven straight over from the team's training camp facility in Mount Charleston. "It's what friends do. You would do the same, and, actually, you have."

"And I recall you didn't appreciate it all that much." It was a careful reference to how affronted Charlotte had been when she'd discovered Joey had used FBI connections to excavate Nate Franco's past—because Charlotte's history with men wasn't exactly glowing.

"Turns out, it was for the best."

Yeah, if *for the best* meant stumbling upon a sophisticated illegal gambling ring that had yet to lead an almighty kingpin to justice. But she wouldn't harp on that now. "Charlotte, this is a date in a library. I've engaged in riskier hookups than this. So far I'm underwhelmed, but I'll be fine."

"Underwhelmed?"

"Just a feeling I have that my life won't change a damn iota once I meet mystery guy. And to think I waxed it bald for this."

"Waxed it bald." Charlotte's mouth twisted in a smirk.

"Well, I'm an optimist."

"About the location. You told me it was his idea to meet here. A library's probably one of the least romantic spots in this city."

"Beg to differ there. The brain's the absolute sexiest organ. Get that stimulated and...wow."

Charlotte blinked. "The brain? Aren't you all about the cock?"

Joey's laughter attracted a few unappreciative glares from the flow of people exiting the gallery. She silenced the outburst but didn't apologize. Walking inside with Charlotte following close, she cataloged all the faces she found. Unless her mystery match had lied about his appearance— six-six, dark hair, dark eyes, beard—he hadn't yet arrived and was late. "I thought I was supposed to be the bad influence in this friendship, but here you are making me disturb the peace. If you get me escorted out of here I can't promise that I'll ever forgive you."

"Is this your not-so-subtle way of asking me to get lost?"

Was he going to show up at all? Had he somehow gotten a look at her and changed his mind about this whole thing?

She didn't want her bride-to-be bestie to be hanging around doling out sympathy once it became undeniably clear that she'd been stood up.

"Charlotte Blue, get lost." Joey lowered onto a bench but continued to register each new face that crossed the threshold. As more people drifted inside, body heat rose and thickened the air. "I should text him, let him know I'm here...waiting."

"Good idea." Charlotte hesitated as Joey opened her pocketbook. "Jo, that's not your phone."

"Bingo!" Joey whispered sarcastically. "This is a junk phone. Keeps things secure."

"Are you ever *not* in federal agent mode?"

"It's who I am." *It's all I am. All I know how to be.*

With a decisive jab, she sent a message.

I'm in the gallery.

The phone vibrated in her palm.

I know you are. You still look good, Jo.

Adrenaline surged as she mutely stood and clutched the walking stick. Her blind date was supposed to be a stranger, but somehow he knew her…knew to call her *Jo*.

Knew how to slip into a room undetected and hide in plain sight.

But the ability to vanish like a vapor when he didn't want to be found was only one of Zafir Ahmadi's exceptional talents.

Across the gallery, he was physically close but their hearts were galaxies apart. Five years had passed since Zaf had curled her naked body against his, since his voice had penetrated every particle of her, since she'd caught the silky strands of his inky black hair between her lips and come at the command of his touch.

His image started to blur, as though he was a figment of her most masochistic fantasy. But there was no hallucination to be blamed, just the stinging mist of tears.

He was real and he was here, though he had no right to be.

Beside her, Charlotte caught sight of him and was subdued to momentary silence. Zaf had that pupil-flaring, panty-wetting effect on women. "Hey, Joey, is that him? Your date?"

The tears danced in Joey's eyes and with a slow blink she set them free. "That's the man who shot me."

Chapter 3

Zaf Ahmadi was a hollow man. Selling his soul for the sake of a vendetta had been a necessary trade—one he didn't resent and wouldn't apologize for. The end—avenging his cousin Raphael's murder—would justify the means.

But Joey should've never been caught in the middle of his war. She was his to protect, and he blamed himself for hurting her. Firing his weapon in an Arizona parking garage hadn't been a mistake, but striking her...loving her... had.

Tried and convicted as an adult on criminal hacking charges when he was a teenager, trained in the US military at the end of his years-long sentence and unleashed in black ops as an emotionally vacant sharpshooter, he was destined for an isolated, tortured life—but Josephine de la Peña had drawn him toward a utopia he'd never known existed. She was light and color and hope, and he'd screwed up and fallen in love with her.

Then his gun, his bullet, his error, had sent her to the ground on a blanket of her own blood, and he'd been slung back to the world he was meant for—a world void of everything he'd known with Joey. She had been shot but it was he who'd fallen off the grid for five damn years.

The single reason he'd come out of the shadows was to protect her. He'd wounded her, wrecked her in some sense, but it hadn't been his plan. That plan belonged to another architect, and Zaf would let no one take her life.

He'd been in Las Vegas some months now, lying low but learning the characteristics of the city and the hierarchy of its people. He surfaced at casinos on the occasions that he wanted to play his intellect against sophisticated dealers ruling high-risk table games.

Mostly he tracked the bastard who'd made Joey his target. The threat to her had intensified to the point that Zaf could no longer effectively watch over her from a distance. He needed access, proximity, trust.

Good friggin' luck getting even one of the three.

Not that he would blame Joey if she tried to run him through with her cane right now. He'd taken no sadistic pleasure in her pain, but welcomed her retaliation. He figured he deserved the wrath, and secretly he prayed it would assuage his agony.

Zaf stood motionless. It was up to her to come to him now. He'd done all the heavy work to this point, hacking into Dating Done Smart's system, creating a profile and neatly bridging it to hers without leaving a trace that security had been breached. This wasn't a federal job—he'd find no governmental cooperation should the company be alerted and take up arms against him. But he didn't care. He knew an attack was coming and this time he would keep her safe.

Inside he shook with a craving to clear the damn room

of everyone but his Jo. *His Jo.* She wasn't anymore—when would that fact take root?

A line of people nudged past him for a closer look at an exhibit, then he could see Joey's tears again. No longer offering a mesmerizing shine to the bitter snap in her russet-brown eyes, they streaked down her cheeks. The woman next to her held out tissues but he wanted to block them with his body and erase the wet trails with his tongue.

Whatever she said next had her friend reaching out as though to shield her, but Joey jerked loose and said something that sent the other woman out of the gallery. Identifying her was no challenge—he knew Charlotte Blue was a Las Vegas Slayers athletic trainer and Nate Franco's fiancée.

And he knew Nate Franco's godfather, Gian DiGorgio, was a billionaire Joey had crossed. He should be in prison now, staring at the blood on his hands. But his brilliance, duplicity and mighty alliances afforded him the slickest loopholes to escape the consequences of his crimes, and gifted him the opportunity to put Joey under surveillance because he intended to lay his bloodstained hands on her.

Joey navigated the gallery to him but didn't speak.

To take the coward's way, he'd ignore the stick, pretend he didn't feel a bone-deep stab of remorse with each halting step he watched her take. But to be a coward required him to fear something, and the capacity to do even that had been drained from him. "I did that. I did that to you."

"You did. The bullet's still embedded. Fragmented. But I'm sure somebody in the network told you that." Those eyes were relentless—punishing, even. Her accent was spiced with the influence of her Spanish-speaking family and Texas upbringing, her timbre controlled and nonthreatening. Deceptively so. "*Qué pasa*, Zaf? How does it feel, knowing you're in me?"

He was beyond redemption for tensing up in violent,

dirty lust. Gazing down at her, he absorbed her every erotic detail. Maybe this *was* punishment, the need to pull those little combs out of her brandy hair and spear his fingers through it, to hurt with a thirst to taste her again, to have perfect vantage point of her breasts exposed by that deep-cut neckline—and knowing he could only need and hurt and look.

"I carry part of you with me wherever I go. I had two surgeries because I wanted you out of my body. But you can't be extracted." She circled him and faced the wall, feigning interest in a painting.

Turning with her, he bumped her and instinctively fitted his hands over her shoulders. Contact. He hadn't been prepared for the naturalness of her frame under his palms and her scent under his nose…the slow and calculated stroke of her ass as she leaned forward on the cane. "Josephine—"

"You didn't answer my question. How does it feel?"

If this was a pressure tactic, he expected something cleverer from her but could make some concessions. "Soft," he murmured against one ear. He scraped her hair aside to access the other. "Familiar. I worshipped this. I've missed it."

"I meant, how does it feel to know you hurt me?"

"Like a mistake I can't undo."

"Not never-ending death?"

"Is that what you want me to feel, Jo?"

A snicker had them looking sideways where a handful of twentysomethings were openly watching them with goofy-as-hell smiles on their faces.

"We can't talk here," he whispered.

"You knew we wouldn't be able to. But you went to shady extremes to get me here, anyway—which is pretty high on the creep-o-meter." Joey straightened her posture and without warning pivoted away, leaving him standing there with a stiff cock and as hooked on her as he'd ever been.

So she was furious and she needed space. He gathered his focus again, striding out of the gallery and putting her back into his line of vision.

Where are you leading me? he wanted to ask, but she was too far ahead, and to raise his voice in a library and be shushed might detonate his temper.

Pursuing the stacks, he watched her disappear down an aisle. Rows of nonfiction books confronted him as he followed her to the end then down the next aisle. She spied him over her shoulder, raised a hand to drag her fingers along the spines of the books but continued on.

It was déjà vu, this chase. They'd shared this dance before. Now did she realize why he'd suggested they meet inside a library? Did she remember what he could never forget?

Sensing the next aisle was empty, he listened for voices but the only close sound he heard was the tap of Joey's cane. Awareness slowed her footsteps and the bounce of her fingertips on the books. Midway she all but stopped, but he kept his casual pace until he was standing before her. Barely turning, she put her backside to the shelves and as she began to drop her hand, he caught it.

Sliding his fingers between hers in an intimate grip, he held her loosely against the bookstack. "We met in a place like this."

He'd been coming off a trafficking assignment in Russia when his supervisors had put him on an aircraft bound for Mexico to join a DEA team. The group had assembled in a library off-hours and during the late-night briefing a petite, fiercely beautiful operative had laid claim to him with just one appreciative smile as he proffered her a thermos of coffee she hadn't asked for but he'd sensed she needed.

He didn't regret sharing weak coffee with Joey that tense night, or joining her afterward for a bottle of tequila and sex in a threadbare room with unscreened windows that let in voracious mosquitos and the fragrance of Mexican orange blossoms.

"I remember," she said, rolling her lips between her teeth as his other hand sought those old-fashioned little combs. Her hair poured over her shoulders like deep-gold citrus honey from a Mason jar—and smelled as sweet. "I remember how we started and how we ended."

A gunshot had ended them. So had his lies.

Zaf hadn't deserved her in the beginning and sure as hell didn't deserve her now, but he was too selfish to deprive himself of the chance to touch her where he knew her olive-toned skin was smoothest and softest. He wanted to shut down all his senses except touch, wanted to know if her subtle warmth and the rhythm of her heartbeat under his hand would heal his gaping wounds. Intently he searched her face for rejection that didn't come.

That first brush of his knuckles down that open trail at the front of her dress almost weakened him to uselessness. Watching her, he saw her lashes tremble and her lips press together.

She wasn't the glittering young woman who tasted like tequila and could strip off her inhibitions grinding out a salsa on an overcrowded dive bar's sticky dance floor. She wasn't even the dogged special agent who fearlessly went deep undercover but always returned to him to remind that good still existed in this goddamn world.

She looked the same and rendered the same savagely primitive effect on his body, but she'd changed.

Skimming his knuckles upward, he curled his fingers around the chain of her purse.

"Shy, Zaf?"

He didn't find the boldness in her tone authentic but accepted the words as a gauntlet thrown. He wasn't shy; he was desperate and venturing into trouble he couldn't mend.

Zaf leaned, angled his head, and she met him halfway.

Her glossy lips were slippery under his kiss, teasing him as if she was flicking a feather across his face.

"Can't seem to make a solid landing there, can you?" she uttered against his mouth.

The *almost* and *not quite* and close misses were a game to her.

But not to him. For Zaf, this was life and death.

"Joey…"

"Shh. Tell me something. You hacked Willa Smart's company to get to me. Was it for this, for a kiss from a woman you used to screw?"

He'd done it because he was her protector. Compromising a matchmaker's compatibility program was the means he'd taken to fulfill his obligation to her. Even if he'd lost his morality, he still possessed a sense of duty—whether he wanted it or not. "You were more than that. You've always known it."

"Have I?"

The love that had once breathed between them had been inconvenient and confusing, yet the realest element in either of their lives. It had struck them unexpectedly. Neither was willing to let it go, and for that they were both to blame. Because something that good couldn't last. Not for people like them who'd done what they had.

"I got to you because I'm on a job," he told her. Yeah, it was a vague explanation, but he wouldn't divulge particulars now. "The kiss is because I can't fight it. I've thought about you constantly since that night. It hasn't been never-ending death, but it's been a never-ending mindfuck."

"They put you down, didn't they? DC?"

"It needed to happen."

"Down deep, Zaf. You didn't turn up at your parents' place in Jersey or even in Pakistan. There was talk that you were dead but I didn't think that. I knew you wouldn't get time, either, that they'd rather have you on reserve than in a cell. About a year after… What I'm trying to say is I tried to bring you back and I couldn't find you."

His mind spun through the past five years. The US government had dragged his ass up for a few missions that needed a sharpshooter of his caliber on the front line, but had thrown him back afterward at his request. He was freelance—off record, off the FBI's payroll, damn near a ghost. He wanted it that way.

"Why'd you want to bring me back?"

"To ask you why you went dirty. You cut a deal with those bastards when I thought we were on the same side. You *killed* me when you turned, damn it."

So she still believed he'd defected to the drug-funneling terrorists he'd been quietly hunting since they'd captured, tortured and murdered his cousin eight years ago. The feds hadn't gone out of their way to clean up his image, but what did it matter now? There was so much that Joey didn't know. But she'd been a thread in a web that was bigger than DEA and even now it was necessary to lead her with lies.

"The kiss," she said finally as fresh tears welled. "Don't fight it."

There was something he didn't altogether trust about her spurring him on, but as he'd said—he couldn't fight it. Nor would he try. Giving her what she provoked, he let go of her hand to hold her head steady. She yielded, opening her mouth to bring him home.

Her taste became his, the slick stroke of her tongue as necessary to him as oxygen. No borders had been settled, so he let himself roam. Parting the halves of her dress, he bared a pair of firm tits. Palming them, preparing them for his mouth, he grazed a nipple with his tongue before catching it in a sucking kiss.

Zaf felt the pressure of her nails burrowing into the back of his neck, but when he started to retreat she pushed him closer. Gasping harshly as his teeth met her flesh, she said, "It doesn't feel the same. Why doesn't it feel the same?"

We're not the same. But he'd be damned if he let that defeat him.

He unwrapped her hand from the cane and set the stick against the books beside them. Guided her to lean back. "Open your legs. Put…" He picked up her hand, selected the middle finger. "This one. Put it inside you."

"Uh…"

Zaf dove for her, touching his nose to hers before covering her mouth in a kiss. "Inside you, Jo."

Pulse hammering, he watched. When she slid her skirt up, exposing the slim thighs that had once straddled him, heat surged. When her hand disappeared beneath the fabric, he said something filthy that drew a private, sexy chuckle. "Are you wet?"

She nodded.

"Say it."

"All right." She flattened her lips, and her cheeks flushed an irresistible dusky color. Now who was shy? "I'm wet."

"Show me."

Joey withdrew her hand, held it up to him. The digit that had been inside her was glazed. As if she knew what he'd demand next, she ran her finger along his mouth. And when he parted his lips to take in the salty-sweet dampness, he gently snapped his teeth over her fingertip and coaxed it deeper before letting her pull out.

"I want more of this," he said.

She shook her head, pushing his chest so she could have room to fix her dress. "I can't. My body's hot for you, but I can't stand here half-naked—"

"Now you're modest?"

"Maybe it's not modesty. Maybe it's decency."

"Oh. So now, all of a sudden, you and I are decent people?"

"I can't pretend that sex will make everything all better. Can you?" Without allowing him the opportunity to approach the question, she tugged him forward to reverse their positions. Now his back was to the stacks and she was leaning against him for balance as she unfastened his belt. "Do you feel the way you felt when I touched you before?"

Zaf was too riveted to comprehend what she was doing. He was staring at her determined frown and the tears collecting in her eyes. Then his pants were open and her fingers were sliding through his pubic hair to wrap around his dick. The first tug of her slim, soft-skinned hand had him bending his knees and groaning out loud.

"Quiet, Zaf," she whispered, establishing a slow-stroke pace and rocking with him. "We're in a library."

"Hold on—"

"Precisely what I'm doing." Her smile was contradicted by the visceral hurt shadowing her face. She didn't interrupt the tempo, but kept attentively working his cock. As fluid coated the tip, she made a satisfied little noise then rubbed it onto her thumb and sucked it. "You taste the same. But something's different. You *know* it's different between us."

Stop her. Get control of yourself.

"This works out nicely for you, Zaf. You betray me, hide for five years, thwart my attempt at something new with a guy who *hasn't* single-handedly destroyed my universe and I get you off, anyway." Joey pressed her face against his shirt to stifle a sob.

Of their own accord his hips gyrated, and he cursed himself for it. How could he still be hard, how could he want this, when she was crying and all but turned inside out? She might be capable of decency now, but he certainly wasn't.

He didn't break away and she kept jerking his shaft until the friction twisted between them and his tension splintered. Teeth gritted, restraint bent, he spurted into her fist. What she didn't capture trickled onto his thighs.

Oh, hell.

"Funny thing about all this," Joey went on, considering her semen-slickened hand and then cleaning it with a few meticulous licks. "It changes nothing. I will *never* forgive what you did to me."

Zaf, still coming down from a sex high, was in a haze as she placed his hand to a spot on her lower abdomen.

"This is the entry point, where your bullet struck me before it cracked my femoral head."

The words dropped him fast, and if he had a heart it'd be as jagged as broken glass right now. "Jo, it was an accident."

"There are no accidents, Archangel." Sweeping up her cane and leaning to kiss him, she left tears on his jaw. "I'm done with you."

Joey escaped to the restroom. At the sink she frantically snatched too many paper towels from the dispenser, splashed too much tepid water and tried to cleanse away the evidence of what she'd done with Zaf. The soap smelled sterile and the towels rasped her skin, but she scoured at her breasts and then her lips, anyway.

The door opened and a woman in a UNLV hoodie and jeans shuffled in as Joey was spitting a soap-and-water mixture into the sink. "Yuck—that can't taste good," she commented. "Hey, are you sick or something?"

Depends. Would you consider giving an ex a handjob in Nonfiction sick?

Joey yanked out more towels to dry her face. Reflected in the mirror were tearful eyes, a rosy-tipped nose and a swollen, blotchy mouth. "I'm good." Lies.

"Sure?"

"Absolutely." Lies. "Thanks."

The woman pursued a stall and Joey slipped outside.

As of right now, this minute, I'm a matchmaker-free zone.

She must be allergic to normal run-of-the-mill sort of meet cutes that led to relationships and love. To keep things in perspective, she hadn't agreed to this date for the prospect of a long-term relationship or love. Still, it cut a little too deep to recognize that at age thirty-three, she was as god-awful at blind-dating as she'd been at age twelve.

She'd arrived at the library with her eyes wide open. She simply hadn't entertained the thought that she would be dealing with Archangel. Zafir Ahmadi was a self-sacrificing guy capable of infinite compassion—contrary to what he wanted to believe. But Archangel, his codename, represented an expert marksman with the heart of a vigilante.

Joey loved Zaf. She hated Archangel.

Archangel was obsessed with revenge. He had overtaken the man she loved. Only, she hadn't seen the signs until that vexed night in Arizona. The narcotics case had put her entire team on edge, so she hadn't noticed that in the days immediately preceding, Zaf had begun to pull away from her. They'd shared meals, fucked, slept wrapped around each other—but the talking had stopped. On that bad night Zaf had turned against their unit and she'd been so jarred that she hadn't protected herself. Someone else's gun had threatened her life, yet it was Zaf's 9 mm bullet that had torn through her.

The precautions, training and Kevlar hadn't shielded her, not really. No armor had covered that vulnerable strip of lower abdomen. Nothing had even stopped her heart from breaking.

The shot had been meant for the man who'd seized her, but she had ignored Zaf's signals because she didn't trust him. Failed signals, miscommunication, and ultimately the sharpshooter had pinned her at close range and she lay crumpled on the ground scarcely aware of the bloody chaos around her.

That had been the last time she'd seen Zaf, until he'd decided to invade the new life she was trying to build here in Nevada.

At least Joey wasn't paranoid. The wariness that warned she was being followed had been perfectly on the mark. Only, this wasn't the kind of thing she was happy to be right about.

Zaf had eyes on her, but why?

Outside again, beneath a canopy of heavy clouds, Joey wasn't entirely surprised to see him on the front entrance steps. He wasn't the type to tuck his tail and run when a mission was on the line. Besides, he owed her a hell of an explanation.

Resting against the handrail, he looked at her with steady intensity. Had what they'd shared not quite twenty minutes ago affected him? It left her a little embarrassed and a lot aroused, reminiscent of when she'd picked open his locker at their Washington, DC, office and tucked her undies inside. "Still here, huh? Did you come for the mind games but stay for the books?"

"I came for you and I stayed for you."

"Yeah, you *did* come for me, Zaf. In a couple of ways. The more pressing issue should be how quickly you can get yourself into a pair of clean pants, yet you're still here angling for a way to get something from me. Single-minded, much?"

Zaf straightened to his full height; he towered over her but somehow it hadn't mattered before. "I want you to let me do my job."

God, the man was prince of the cloak-and-dagger. "Which is what?"

"Protecting you."

Joey halted, taking a moment to seek out the lie in his face, but she couldn't break through. She saw a man she'd missed even as she cursed the sweltering summer day she'd met him seven years ago. All she could seem to attach herself to were the memories of lazy conversations and how he altruistically volunteered his life for the law. Lean and carelessly sexy with that serious, brooding look that magnetized people even as it pushed them away, he was the Zaf her heart recognized.

But the guy who'd manipulated her into a confrontation? That screamed Archangel. It was his modus operandi.

"Goodbye, Zaf." She skirted around him to the other side of the handrail.

"Wait, please," he said, matching her steps but keeping the rail between them. "You can't look me square in the eye and say you haven't wondered if somebody's tailing you."

"Yes, I've wondered." She'd also wondered if paranoia was making her crazy. "Now I know I was right and the doer is you."

"It's not me—"

"Actually," she said, eyes narrowed as she looked around them, "the old guy with the ratty corduroy pants and the Copernicus biography. Is he on your payroll? Because I'd hate to think I handed a one-hundred-dollar bill to one of your spies."

"No, I didn't recruit spies." He wasn't even fazed that she'd accused him of it. That'd probably disturb some, but putting extra sets of eyes on subjects was a common investigative practice in their world. "You gave a hundred dollars to a beggar?"

"I don't know if he was a beggar for certain, but figured the money would cut him some slack. So I'll skip my next manicure. I don't mind."

"You're a beautiful person, Jo, with beautiful intentions.

But don't you think cash like that might go toward heroin in his veins instead of food in his stomach?"

"I saw the good in him. Sometimes a person needs someone else to see the good in them, Zaf." With that she was back on the move.

"Josephine, hang on for a minute, okay?"

"No, I don't have time for this. I'm getting along fine and the sooner you disappear again, the better."

"Do you mean that?"

"I do." Lies, lies, lies. But they were her strength and comfort because he couldn't be trusted with the truth. "I have friends here and a stable job at ODC. Plus, as you're damn well aware, I'm testing out the dating scene. So I have no time for your pretenses. I don't want you anymore."

The last few words crackled in the muggy air. "I might believe that had I not been in that library with your hand around my cock."

Oh, sure. Bring *that* up. She stabbed her cane to the step. "Hey, you don't get to crawl out of the woodwork when I'm trying to patch up my life. And you, of all folks, don't get to judge me. So give your so-called protection to someone who wants it."

That shut him down, but only for a taut moment. He literally jumped the rail, his feet touching down neatly on the step below hers.

"How impressive, you do your own stunts." Thank goodness for snark—dishing it out gave her time to push past a tide of arousal. Facing him full-on took her breath away.

Zaf leaned close, kissed her cheek for the benefit of people passing them on the stairs. To strangers they appeared to be a normal pair of lovers relishing the brightness of each other's company on a dreary afternoon. So far from the truth. "Joey, you're wearing a target."

"Who put it there?" Asking the question didn't mean she had to put stock in what he said. It wouldn't be the first time he lied to achieve an end result.

"Gian DiGorgio."

"Are you lying?" He wasn't; she fully and completely trusted that on this occasion he was honest. God-given instincts, sharpened by a career as a federal agent, had made her suspicious of coincidences. It wasn't by chance that in recent weeks Gian DiGorgio repeatedly appeared at the bodega where she'd shopped for years and had never before seen him. Happenstance wasn't at work when she visited the post office and found the man twisting a key into the box next to hers. Though the Bureau lent her a few courtesies, she had no recourse against a citizen exercising his rights to patronize a bodega and keep a post office box.

But to doubt Zaf would pressure him to release information he likely was reluctant to share with her yet—if at all.

"I'm not lying, Jo."

Just to stress that she wouldn't allow herself to be handled, she said, "I want proof."

"I'll get it to you."

"Good."

"Look, I know you don't trust me, but DiGorgio isn't some playground bully. This isn't casual advice between old friends. Eliminating the threat to your life is my job. Once before you pissed on my judgment, and neither of us will forget how that played out."

Joey flinched. "This conversation's over."

"Take this seriously," he pleaded. "I didn't come to Las Vegas to dig up the past or make you cry or to blame you for my screwups."

"Really? Seems that way to me."

"None of it was intentional. You're no longer an irritation to DiGorgio—you're a threat. I've had him tagged for the past few months. What he wants with you is personal. From what I've gathered, he's willing to handle you himself."

Inside Joey was cold, and anxiety slammed her so hard that her spine started to ache. But she said indifferently, "Let him give it a try, then. Gian DiGorgio's kissing seventy and he's no he-man. I can cope."

"There's a difference between being strong and being stupid."

"No one asked you to be my rescuer, Zaf." She waited for a retort—his body language said he was burning to argue—but no words came and she shrugged. "Give me whatever intelligence you've collected."

"I want to talk to you about this more."

In other words, he wanted control. But it was she who wore a target. Her life rested in her own hands. That hadn't changed just because he decided to swagger back into it.

"Come to the house tonight, about sevenish. I'm sure you already know exactly where it is. Bring beer. I like it light these days." She wouldn't be home, but let him figure that out in time.

"Okay." He turned to jog down the steps but hesitated. "Hey, Jo."

"What?"

He might've tried for a smile, but it curved into a contemplative frown. God, she'd been a fool to love him once. A delightfully buoyant little fool. Not anymore, though, and that might be the saddest thing of all. "Nothing. See you tonight."

"Tonight," she confirmed, sending him off with a smile she didn't feel.

Pulling out her phone—not the junk one, which was safe to pitch into a receptacle now, but her smartphone—she found missed calls and unread texts waiting. She'd manage Charlotte's grilling later. She owed her friend an explanation after dropping a doozy of a bomb on her in the lobby gallery earlier, but she needed an urgent favor and knew who could get it done.

"Tem, hi," she said cheerily when the woman picked up the call. Pleasantries out of the way, she asked, "About that car. Is the offer still on the table? 'Cause I'm going to do an overnight at the training facility and I could use a change of wheels. With the veterans reporting to camp tomorrow, I should get my bearings. Let's make that happen tonight, shall we?"

Tem agreed to make the necessary arrangements and, hanging up, Joey grappled for some sort of inner reassurance that using the Las Vegas Slayers gig to dodge Zaf was wise. He would worry about her until he found her again.

But she supposed if she could manage that burden for five years, then surely he could shoulder it for a single night.

Decision final, Joey slid into her Camaro and headed home to pack.

Chapter 4

So this was what it was like to be a Blue for a night.

As she was working a case and now obligated to view things through a professional lens, Joey made a dedicated effort to see the car as a mere tool that would enable her to complete an assignment with utmost efficiency.

And style. Sexy, sinful, magnificent style.

But the Ferrari that had been practically white-glove delivered in front of her property was not the transportation of mere middle-class mortals. It was black fire screaming for attention in a sedate suburban *Stepford Wives* neighborhood. A dark devil disturbing a congregation of luminous angels.

The sensible town car on the curb, where one of the Blues' drivers sat stoically at the wheel, was more suitable for someone in her tax bracket and who sampled the celebrity experience whenever her high-profile friendships drew her into that realm. As she moved aside to clear a path on the front walk for the man who'd handed her the envelope containing the Ferrari's keys and papers and was carrying out her travel bag to stow in the trunk, she wondered if she could negotiate a change.

But Tem would hear none of that. "Appreciate the car, Josephine. If it causes any physical discomfort, then let me know."

Joey retreated to a trio of palm trees in her front yard and watched the men drive off in the other car. In all likelihood Tem had emergency-texted them to take off pronto. "The thing is this. Contrary to what Hollywood action movies depict, special agents don't drive six-figure luxury cars."

"Seven."

"What?"

"It was an auction find my husband impulse-bought in Europe. He paid seven figures, got bored and it's been under tarp for ages."

Joey had to stare at her phone for a moment. *The behaviors of the rich and mighty never cease to blow my friggin' mind.* "Well, I feel slightly less unworthy knowing you didn't go to much expense on my account, but it's not practical for someone like me."

Tem gave a long-suffering sigh. "Listen to you. *Unworthy. Someone like me.* What makes you any less deserving than anyone else? It's transportation, not a key to infinite power. It was made to be driven and since you're traveling to Mount Charleston on account of the Las Vegas Slayers, it's Marshall's and my responsibility to see to it that you're well equipped to handle your responsibilities. Besides, it's only a loaner. We fully expect it to be returned to us in the condition that it arrived."

"So I should Hoover out the cookie crumbs and toss all the fast-food wrappers before giving you back the keys?"

Tem's gentle breathing filled the line for a stretched moment. "You've been eating in the car? Already? I'll send you the contact information for the company that details our vehicles."

"For cripe's sake, I'm just joking." Joey laughed at Tem's relieved gasp.

"My apologies, Josephine. Perhaps it's because you and I are from different generations, but I'm one for whom *jokes* are meant to be funny. I've never understood how you can wear sarcasm all the time."

"I'd feel naked without it."

"And there it is, once again."

"Yes, I know. That one was specially for you." Noting the time, she made tracks for the Ferrari. Casting a glance at the garage that housed her Camaro, she supposed it had earned time off. It wasn't as though she was trading it in for a ride that was laughably outside her means. "I'm driving over to the training facility now. I'll get in touch tomorrow with my impression."

"Oh—speaking of impressions, please tell me you aren't planning to show up there in a variation of what you wore to dinner at CUT."

She sank into the driver's seat and almost moaned. Recovering, she said, "Not quite. Jeans and tank. There are no practices tonight, so I imagine your men will be unwinding. I thought it'd be more strategic to keep things casual tonight while they're relaxing with their guards down, and reserve the business attire for a more professional impression at orientation tomorrow."

"Well. That make sense. Startlingly so."

That was no compliment. "I have a way of making sense sometimes. Your shock is disconcerting if not off-putting. Are you surprised that *Eliza Doolittle* might be competent, after all?"

"It wasn't the kindest comment I could've made, I'll agree," Tem acknowledged, but she didn't seem all that contrite.

"Why did you choose me, then?"

"It's very practical, really. Since you're ex-DEA, you have an in that can benefit my company. That you're Charlotte's closest—and I'd venture to say most loyal—friend, makes you an excellent choice. You wouldn't see our team face the embarrassment of media outcry if it would negatively impact her. It's simply your way, and your way is of use to us."

How would Tem react to learn that Joey's loyalty to the Blues came with dangerous consequences? Would she still consider Joey of use or rather an unnecessary liability? From what she'd observed when each of Marshall and Tem's daughters had slipped into a messy situation, the patriarch and matriarch tended to favor Slayers damage control over all else—so chances of seeing them defend her in any fashion were pathetically slim.

But, as Joey had insisted to Zaf, she didn't ask for protection. Nor would she. Joey had acted in the right, knocking over the first domino that brought down the unregulated gambling network and game-fixing Gian DiGorgio was running with Nate Franco's father, Alessandro. DiGorgio had a duty to operate his businesses within the confines of the law. Franco had a duty to protect the Las Vegas Slayers under his ownership. Their machinations were to blame for DiGorgio's crumbling empire and Franco's last resort to sell the franchise to the Blues. DiGorgio remained under federal scrutiny and Franco's current residence was a psychiatric hospital, but if either man had grievances against her, then she would manage them on her own.

Somehow.

DiGorgio had been arrested for putting a price on Franco's head, but then the guy had attempted suicide before the hit could be executed. And disturbingly enough, only a few weeks ago the would-be hit man had recanted his confession before taking his leave.

Joey glanced down the street in one direction then the next. Damn Zaf for eliminating the hope that she was safe, for opening the Pandora's box of debilitating fear that had her checking her home security system and taking her sidearm out of storage for cleaning.

"Drive safely, Josephine."

"Fine, no *Die Hard* high-speed chases." This time the other woman gave in to a chuckle. "Tem, I do intend to complete this job successfully. I'd advise you to rest assured, but I know you won't."

Neither will I.

"At least there's a full-size bed." Joey wasn't expecting an answer. She stood alone in her ten-by-twelve standard single room at the Slayers' training facility, Desert Luck Center. Considering very little expense appeared to have been spared in the design of the state-of-the-art buildings and striking outdoor space, she'd counted on a hotel vibe but found the sleeping quarters utilitarian and dormitory-esque. The rooms had been painted in neutral tones and decorated with a decidedly masculine scheme in mind. She was grateful that housekeeping had made an attempt to personalize the space before her last-minute arrival. The vibrant bouquet on the dresser was almost captivating enough to mask the woodsy scent of the plug-in air freshener, which she tugged out of the electrical outlet before stretching out across the silver-and-Slayers-red plaid-covered bed.

The mattress could benefit from a pillow top, but it would suffice for one night. She supposed working a desk job for four years had spoiled her. While in DC she'd kept a pillow and blanket on site to nap on the floor, and during field assignments she'd taken sleep wherever she could find it. On the nights she was with Zaf, the comfort of his body had been all she needed to sink into deep, undisturbed dreams.

The easy way her mind drifted to the man had her sitting up and shaking her head as if to reorganize her thoughts.

So carefully she had conditioned herself to shut down every beautiful memory of him and who she'd been when she had him in her life. He'd been her man, her love, the strength she felt elated to know was there should she need him.

That man didn't exist anymore. Had he ever?

It was a question she wasn't in the mood to contemplate. She was Quantico trained, had exceptional intellectual ability and wasn't weak-willed enough to allow him to distract her from the work she'd been hired to do at Desert Luck Center.

Joey unpacked quickly and devoted a few necessary minutes to reviewing the information she'd collected about NFL policies and the Las Vegas Slayers specifically. Since agreeing to help the Blues identify the recreational drug users on their squad, she had been digging into research from player files to social media profiles to training regimens.

Because the Slayers' random drug testing historically was quite predictable for any weed-smoker who didn't want to be found out—once a year, typically during training camp when the full roster was first gathered before the start of a season—she suspected all men would wait until midcamp to get high. It wasn't unheard of, certainly wasn't the only means to beat a drug test, and across the league there seemed to be an unspoken understanding that this was a common practice.

Though she'd remain watchful, she didn't expect to have names at the ready until after the Slayers' testing commenced in August. That allowed her time—not much, a few weeks—to *build a rapport*, as Temperance Blue had said.

If any players were to host a weed party to celebrate pissing clean, she needed to be on that guest list. In a manner of speaking her new employers had informed her of precisely this.

Joey touched up her makeup before locking her room and hazarding a sly tour of the building. She made it a priority to memorize who bunked with whom and tried to isolate the earthy smell marijuana left lingering in the air and on fabrics. Sniffing cologne and that damn sandalwood that must be wafting out from every room in the building, she eventually sought the source of noise on the main floor.

The floor plan she'd reviewed previously informed that there were separate recreation rooms designated to players and staff. The one that held over half a hundred males and a sprinkle of female staff members was the players' lounge.

This was the hot spot for the night. Noting the basic surroundings—luxurious leather seating, a spacious kitchen, computer stations and flat-screen TVs offering a range of showings from ESPN to a network-channel sitcom to pay-per-view porn—she joined the gathering in the kitchen.

The men who'd let her through closed the space behind her and she felt as if she was lost in the woods. Most of the players she matched to roster photos were tall with intimidating muscular bulk, but the same could be said for many of Slayers' coaching and training staff. Testosterone pinged off the walls and vibrated in the air.

Catching the eye of another female, this one wearing an employee ID tag, she gave a friendly wave and received an impersonal once-over in return. Okay, so much for girl-to-girl friendship. It wasn't a major loss, as Charlotte was the only friend she expected to encounter at camp, any-

way. Charlotte had made an appearance here this morning and after reporting to the Clark County Library to be
Joey's pillar of support, she'd said she was going home to
her fiancé. That meant Joey was essentially on her own
with strangers, which was a better scenario for what she
hoped to accomplish.

She didn't need Charlotte lingering and questioning
her motives.

To no one specifically, she mentioned, "I was torn between watching the threesome on TV and coming in here
for whatever's baking. Guess I made the right choice."

Grunts and laughter answered her, and someone said,
"Coach's making cookies."

That would be… Joey peered around wide backs and
thick arms as the men jostled each other and turned up
beverages. The chef had blond hair, a ruddy suntan and had
hooked a pair of sunglasses onto his apron. Kip Claussen,
the head coach. She knew the man had been brought on
board when the Blues acquired the team and that he had
a tendency to cuss and break sunglasses.

Looking again at the pair dangling from his apron, she
noticed they were missing an arm and one of the lenses
was cracked.

Giggling, she crossed her arms, poking the man in front
of her. "Oh, sorry," she said when he turned around. "Tight
fit in here."

"Nah, it's cool. *Hola, chica.*"

Joey kept her eyes in the forward position, though
they begged to roll to convey how unimpressed she was
when men attempted to use Spanish—and dreadfully pro-
nounced Spanish, at that—to hit on her.

And "Hey, girl" in English or Spanish never got her hot.

"Damn," the man said, openly appraising her and doing
a double take when he found her cane. Then, upon ultimately deciding the accessory was a nonissue, he turned

on what he must define as *charm* but she'd call *sleaze*. "Baby, what that mouth do?"

"For you, *nada*."

The people whose attention had been on them hooted and catcalled, and she moved along until she'd wiggled her way to the massive counter where the head coach was setting out baking pans.

"Let them cool a few minutes. They're hot enough to burn," he cautioned, but she saw a sea of hands reach out, anyway and promptly heard yelps and exclamations of "Ow, damn it!" and "That's hot!"

"Do you suppose next time they'll believe you, Coach Claussen?" Joey asked, amused.

"No, don't think they will," he predicted with a grim look. The crowd began to separate as some moved into the next room to wait for the cookies to reach a temperature that wouldn't cause bodily harm. "You're Josephine, right?"

"'Fraid so." She smiled, compelled to see if it might be contagious and could break up the man's frown. "Who warned you about me?"

"Marshall and Tem did. Good to meet you." He wiped his large hands on a napkin and in lieu of shaking hers, he gestured for her to join him where he stood near the double oven. Draping an arm over her shoulders, he shifted close to murmur, "I'm aware of why you're really here. They looped me in."

"Then you won't interfere?"

"Do what you gotta do." To the room at large he said, "Yo, everyone. This is Josephine de la Peña. Emails went out about the drug prevention program we've got going through camp. If you didn't get one, find somebody who did. Josephine's from the Office of Diversion Control and she's in on the prevention program with the Good Samaritans of Nevada. So any questions, she's your go-to person. But please, don't ask her where to score the good shit. That's not what she's here for."

"Actually, Kip," she said sweetly, "I'm not official until the presentation at orientation. So at the moment I'm a woman who's eating your food and enjoying free satellite TV."

The response was a mix of friendly laughter and complaints that the front office had implanted a narc into their space.

Kip started lifting cookies off the baking sheets and onto pans. She picked up a chocolate chip cookie and took a bite.

And now for a little test. "Oh, that's good. There are recipes floating around that incorporate alcohol. Rum, bourbon, Guinness—whatever you're after. Not as potent as pot cookies, but they're recreationally legal."

The head coach started to send a frown her way but covered and continued his task. Joey was in tune with everyone in the room, her eyes performing a panoramic scan for changes in expression or stance that indicated interest that hadn't been present before she mentioned pot cookies.

It was a subtle way to send out feelers and see what they'd turn up over the course of the night.

Three cookies and several conversations later, she made her way to the staff lounge and took the liberty of downing half a bottle of water to dilute some of the sugar and caffeine. Kip Claussen and the head athletic trainer— Whitaker Doyle, she believed—were inside consulting schedules over cold beer.

Joey reconsidered her water, but opted to stay faithful and finish it.

Kip introduced her to the trainer, who was on his way out, then stood and stretched, looking at the twilight outside the windows. "Ballsy, what you said in the kitchen. Pot cookies."

"I don't know if anyone will bite. No one's made up their mind about me yet."

"To be on the level here, I haven't made up my mind about you."

"No?"

"No." He strode past her to look out the door, then, leaving it open, he returned to the recesses of the room and signaled her over. "I've been working with the Blues for a year and I like to think I'm familiar with their…managerial style. Maybe they don't cross the line to get things done, but they sure as hell will walk on it."

"What does your judgment say should be done?"

"Eat up the expense of a second random drug test during the season, but the Blues want to avoid midseason lineup changes. They don't want sponsors and the media scrutinizing how our team might handle things if the player happens to be someone we depend on to win games. Now, before game one, is the time to tidy up. If these men are smart, they'll stay clean until after the annual test. Then we could be looking at dealing with somebody who's getting high through the season or potentially putting them in a probationary program for a few months and facing the possibility of more damn drama. So what I'm asking you is if you intend to use entrapment to bump a few high risks off my roster."

She pitched her bottle into a recycling bin and took the seat Whitaker had vacated. "I'm not going to go so far as to solicit drugs to anyone."

"The guys noticed you. And the one who said that disrespectful comment to you is a new recruit, drafted as a tackle. I'll handle him." He relaxed in his chair, linking his fingers behind his head. "Correct me if I'm way off base here, but a lot of men are willing to take on certain personas if it means getting a beautiful woman. Tread carefully if your plan is to put it out there that you smoke or shoot, whatever. A guy who's ruled by his dick will make you think he's into using, too, if it gives him an edge over the rest of the pack."

"Kip, I'm trained to know the difference." She paused as he sat forward and swiped up his MGD for a swig. "You seem unconvinced."

"This team has seen unprecedented crises. A lot of it was inherited from Alessandro Franco's reign, but some came from our own team members. I'm over that and don't want more of it this season."

"And that's why I was hired. Tread carefully, sir, if you're getting a look at me and see only weakness. I'm stronger than I look." She'd need to be to complete this job, return to ODC where she belonged and, of course, keep herself out of a billionaire thug's reach.

Beer finished, Kip crumpled the can and pitched it. "Look, Josephine—"

"Call me Joey."

"Joey. Some of the staff's heading into Vegas for a bite. Why don't you come with us?"

It was an invitation into an inner circle. Not the players', but that would come and this was progress. The Blues had not specifically asked her to put staff under suspicion, but doing so would offer her a more detailed picture.

"Tempting," she said, getting up and squeezing his arm. "I'll have to pass, though. I heard someone issue a foosball challenge. Can't miss that."

"Jesus," he said, scratching his forehead. "They don't stand a freaking chance."

"What's that mean?"

"They're going to fall in love with you."

Watching him leave, she hoped he was wrong. Gathering the hearts of men, nearly all of whom she'd venture to guess were in relationships, was not part of her agenda. Parker Brandt was the last man who'd figured he was in love with her, and their breakup had been messy to the point that they could find no friendship between them anymore.

Besides, the gladiator-like professional athletes she found here seemed to be interested in shallow sexual attraction, and she would do nothing for them in that respect. The Blues had been clear and she wasn't aiming to strike up anything new.

Not after her adventure in blind dating had resurrected her ex.

Don't think about him. Don't let him get to you.

Perhaps it was morbid curiosity, and if it was, Joey didn't particularly care as she forewent the foosball game kicking off in the players' lounge and returned to her room. The blooms' fragrance was stronger now than it'd been when it was competing with chemically engineered sandalwood.

It was after eight, over an hour past the time she'd told Zaf to show up at her place. She'd trashed the disposable phone and though she knew with certainty he had her cell number, she found no calls or texts on the screen.

Taking the phone to the dresser, she breathed in the bouquet's gentle smell and thought it'd neutralize the impact of realizing Zaf wasn't trying to get through to her. Maybe his Rhett no longer gave a damn about her Scarlett.

In the end, she would save herself, so why should she entertain the thought that she might want closure after he dropped off the grid five years ago?

Rubbing her nose against the petal of a gardenia, she closed her eyes. Perhaps she wasn't heartsick for a lover, but homesick for loved ones. She dialed a familiar number.

"Hello?" a masculine voice as rough as unsanded timber greeted.

It was late but Joey pictured Hector de la Peña still tinkering around in the flower shop he shared with his wife.

The family business had been a single store within their small town outside El Paso during Joey's childhood, but had since opened locations throughout Texas. The family had the means to allow both Hector and Anita early retirement, but neither would give up their careers.

Hector was an authority on flowers and his wife ran the books, and that was what Joey—and now, she was quite sure, her younger brother—told anyone who questioned how the de la Peña family could afford one of the most prosperous spreads in their corner of Texas on a florist's salary.

"Hola, Papá. ¿Cómo estás?"

"Josephine! *Hola, mija.* You taking care of yourself?"

"Como siempre."

"Yeah, then why do you sound sad?"

She poured cheer into her voice. "I'm smelling flowers and missing you and Mamá and Eddie and the shop, that's all."

She wouldn't bring her troubles to her family's door. Her mother, Anita, had been a force to be reckoned with in supporting the trajectory of Joey's career in law enforcement.

But Hector was a man of pride and ruled as head of the household. He'd wanted his daughter to become a chef, after noticing her fervor for baking treats to sell in the flower shop. Then he thought she might earn a teaching license and devote her career to TESOL. Then, when she'd announced to the family that her calling was in law enforcement, he'd said he would allow it only if she took the LSATs and failed. If she passed, she would pursue law school and become a lawyer. The thought of her working undercover as a field agent had worried him to the point that it had impacted his health, and she hadn't wanted to openly defy him to pursue the career she'd been meant for since she was a girl.

So she'd lied to him, claiming she failed the LSATs, and he'd given her his blessing to pursue the field.

Gradually, Hector had begun to accept her career—until she'd been shot. Her parents and brother had come to DC for post-op support and then to Las Vegas to make sure she wasn't indulging in what gave the place its Sin City nickname—she was, very enthusiastically—but she hadn't visited Texas in years.

Something Hector reminded her every time they managed to catch each other by phone. "You wouldn't miss us if you came home once in a blue moon, *mija*."

"That's what you say. I think if I came home, I'd only miss you more each time I left. That's no way to live."

"Right. So you should live here, work in the family business. We won't even require an interview."

She smiled. "And leave all this sin and debauchery behind? You're a silly man, Papá."

Hector grumbled, "You think you're being funny when you say stuff like that, but it worries me."

"I don't mean to worry you… Listen, is Mamá around?"

"She's back at the ranch, asleep. Want me to get her to call you? I know when there's something you want to tell Anita that you can't tell me, it's important."

"Don't bother her. It's all right."

"You sure?"

No, she almost blurted. *Zaf Ahmadi is back and I can't be certain everything I felt for him died when he disappeared.*

Except, she'd never given her parents Zaf's name. She had said a colleague had fired during an operation and she'd been unintentionally hit. Clinical. Clean. Unemotional.

"Anita will be sorry she missed you. She'll send me to the couch when she finds out I let her sleep through your call."

"I'll call again—soon. Promise. Tell Eddie I'm thinking about him." She hesitated, touching the phone as if to
lay a hand on his cheek. "Papá, don't work too hard. *Dale
un beso a Mamá de mi parte. Te extraño.*"

"*Buenas noches, mija.*"

Speaking to Papá, hearing the concern and uncondi-
tional love in his voice, never ceased to leave Joey with
a scratchy sensation of guilt. She hated lying to him. But
she lied to protect him and for years had been searching
for ways to be at peace with that.

Drawn out of her room again, she declined a defensive
lineman's suggestion for a fast hookup in his room and went
downstairs to the ruckus of revelry in the players' lounge.

She hesitated to infiltrate. She wanted the men to main-
tain a sense of a safe place that wasn't threatened by a
narc. So she needed an invitation. A player, preferably
one with tenure on the Slayers' roster, would have clout
and if he vouched for her then she had a better chance of
gaining acceptance.

The starting quarterback would be a bona fide ace in
hand, but Dex Harper wasn't expected to report to camp
until tomorrow morning. The press was obsessed with
his affair with the team's former general manager, Danica
Blue. Joey knew that Dex and Danica were each other's
obsession, and love made them crave private moments
however and whenever they could be found.

To have a man of his status stand by her would be great,
but Joey could do this with a touch of creativity. "I missed
a hard-core foosball game, didn't I?" she said softly from
the entryway, and the man nearest her twisted around holding a bottle of beer topped with a lime wedge.

"You're talking to the champ." He held out a hand and
her gaze followed a trail of eclectic tattoos up his arm to
the cotton shirt stretched across the muscles carved into
his body. A cocky grin and dozens of thin cornrows were

a shot of handsome on such a troubled, severe canvas. His umber complexion wasn't smooth and his hand calloused, but she'd always been more comfortable with rugged, un-refined men.

Laborers similar to her father, who was as much a gardener as he was a scientist, athletes who pushed their bodies to extremes and men who confronted danger with selfless bravery intrigued her.

Shaking his hand, she recognized him now.

You're exactly who I'm looking for, Mr. Dibbs.

TreShawn Dibbs, a twenty-five-year-old in his second season as the Slayer's kicker. Las Vegas had picked him up after San Diego had dropped him for steroid abuse—along with a slew of off-field transgressions. "Congratulations."

"I'm TreShawn," he said, still holding her hand, and she was at risk of blushing at the blatant interest emanating from him. He probably didn't realize he was sending all sorts of flares but she wouldn't embarrass him by calling him on it, especially since she needed him in her corner.

"I know. ESPN has a crush on you," she said, with a smile of her own. "Plus, I know you're Charlotte Blue's friend. As am I."

"Charlotte didn't tell me she had a friend as smokin' as you. That ain't right."

It was such a line, one he'd do better to save for a woman he had a chance of wooing. He was twenty-five to her thirty-three, lived the high life to its fullest and she was unavailable in a multitude of ways.

"Forgive her," Joey said brightly. "I should go. Wouldn't want to bring down everyone's good time."

He faltered, then, "Naw, mostly everybody's chill. The ones who aren't, don't pay them attention. Come in."

"Thanks."

Descending on the lounge, she appreciated that TreShawn was laid-back and didn't feel the need to hover at every moment. Eventually, as one hour drifted to the next, others lowered the drawbridge of mistrust just enough to allow her a glimpse into their personalities. She wouldn't push too hard too fast and had to accept that she'd done what she could as the crowd started to thin.

"Want a breather from the VIP?" TreShawn asked her. "The practice fields aren't that far."

Joey was in flats and her hip could stand some motion. Outside, she quickly paged through her memory bank for league infractions that had been linked to the athlete.

Cocaine possession. If the man had used cocaine and bulked up with steroids, who was to say he'd turned a complete one-eighty and was clean now? Any team member with a history of prior recreational drug use should be looked at closely, and the Blues were right to put him under a microscope.

"So is this camp drug program league-wide?" he asked after a few minutes of silence as they crossed the turf. It all seemed endless—the crisp lawn, the heavenly sky that might be star-dotted if not for the bright field lighting.

"No, this is something Slayers management constructed to keep you men educated and healthy. You don't sound excited about it."

"The thing is, I heard the 'say no to drugs' spiel all through school."

"And how old were you when you started using coke?"

"Are you talking about that possession charge? That was a bad rap. Wasn't mine."

"Okay," she conceded, watching her cane swing forward as she walked. "Then what did you use, and when did you start?"

TreShawn picked up speed and was a yard or so ahead of her when he said without turning back to look her way, "Weed. I was fourteen. I gave it up after I got drafted. Doesn't seem to matter, though. The screwups are all that folks like to remember when they're looking for somebody to blame."

"Are you back on steroids, TreShawn?"

Finally, he turned around. "Hey, I don't owe you any answers."

"I know. But I want them, anyway." She stopped walking when he began to cut away the distance between them as he strode across the field.

Stretching out his arms, then gesturing from his chest to feet, he said solemnly, "This is all me. This season I'm in it to break records."

Diamond rings glittered boldly on his fingers, and the intensity in his tone took her awareness away from the faint smell of sandalwood he carried on his clothes and the hushed rustle of the Mount Charleston breeze.

Blessed Mary, the man was gorgeous. He had the potential to make someone who *wasn't* her very happy.

"What's your next question? Are you thinking I asked you out here to spit some game?"

"I'm thinking it was a friendly offer to take a breather from the VIP. That's what you said. Am I wrong to have trusted you?"

I'm giving you a way to sidestep rejection. Take it.

She nearly exhaled in relief when he said, "A friendly offer. Yeah, that's all this was about. Want to go back now?"

"Okay." She had to let the single word suffice.

When she returned to her room, she lay on the bed and compiled updates to report to the team owners. She stretched out but somehow the position just wasn't comfortable. Lying on her side with her arms wrapped around a pillow, she tried to mute the words that seemed jammed on repeat.

They're going to fall in love with you.

They would know hurt, the same as any other man

who'd tried to find a future with her. She felt undercover again, though this time she wasn't hiding behind a false identity.

Field work had once distracted her with an almost perverse thrill—because for her there'd been no richer high than being deep in a job—but sometimes loneliness and emptiness penetrated, made her desperate. So desperate that she used sex to escape. And so desperate that she'd considered walking away from the FBI, before an errant bullet had made the decision for her.

She couldn't entertain loving a man who didn't understand her world. It was unfathomable that she could rewire herself to love someone the way she loved Zaf before everything between them had fallen apart.

That love didn't exist anymore, and even if it did, the lies and the scars left no room for it now. Her heart was a hostile environment and if she could remember that, then maybe loneliness would stop leaving tears on her pillow.

Chapter 5

Joey couldn't say she was sorry to be dismissed from training camp for the day. It had been a full-throttle morning.
First, she'd observed two Good Samaritans of Nevada
presentations in an overly air-conditioned film viewing
room—one seminar and Q&A session for veterans; the
other for rookies. Then she loitered on the sidelines with
the media as fans finagled autographs and selfies. After
that she'd found Charlotte to set up a girls' night gabfest
then wrapped things up with a catered brunch and Bloody
Mary cocktails with the Blues and Kip Claussen.

None of the conversations she'd overheard among the
athletes the previous night had been drug-centered or concerning otherwise. Overall, the mood had been low-key
and the men easygoing, aside from a heated card game and
some social media back-and-forth.

So she'd need to sharpen her focus and pick out what
wasn't on the surface.

When the media had been cleared off the premises so

propriety team activities could commence, she left, as well, agreeing to meet her supervisor for lunch at Nickel's, a little off-Strip café.

The eggs benedict she'd eaten earlier still had her tummy in a happy place, but as Ozzie Salvinski knew, she wasn't one to pass up free food. Nickel's spectacular Baileys Irish Cream cheesecake would go a long way toward helping her unwind.

Professional football was high-octane, glamorous. It wasn't anything she couldn't handle—she knew her roots and always kept herself grounded—but she'd be lying if she claimed it didn't have its surreal moments. Sports entertainment combined two sides of a coin, sweat and celebrity, and it was fascinating.

Breaking away from it all to shoot the breeze in a linoleum-floored, scratched-countered spot downtown, then going home to a place that embodied neither rough-and-tough sports nor dazzling entertainment would be a welcome change of milieu.

"The Blues outfitted you in that?" From a table with a street view, Ozzie pointed out the window as Joey sat across from him.

Then there was the fact that she'd be driving *that* home. The Ferrari sat in front of its meter looking like lust with a steering wheel.

"That they did," she said, reaching around the toasted submarine sandwich on his tray to pick up the sliced dill pickle. She still wasn't planning on leaving the joint without cheesecake, but dill slices were a guilty pleasure.

"Hey, come on," Ozzie protested as she bit into it with a crunch. "Get the waitress over here and order your own."

"This is all I want. And a slice of Baileys cheesecake." She watched a string of people stop to ogle the car. "It's an incredible set of wheels, but I don't feel like myself when I drive it."

"Learning curve? Maybe you've been stuck in that Camaro too long."

"No, I don't mean that. Marshall Blue bought it as a hobby ride. It looks like something Batman would drive when he's cruising through Gotham trying to pick up women."

Ozzie wrapped a bear paw of a hand around his sandwich. "You've been in good with the Blues for years. All of the flash and money and fame still get to you?"

She chewed thoughtfully. "Sometimes, yes. Charlotte, her sisters, they're down-to-earth gals, which is probably difficult for people to believe since they grew up in luxury. Marshall and Tem, however, they spare no expense." She finished the pickle and took a hand wipe packet off their table's napkin dispenser.

"Isn't your family well-off? You've got good Texas land, purebred horses, the works."

"Well, that's hardly been my life for a while now. I grew up helping out in the flower shop, went to college, took up a career in DEA and lived off my own paychecks since. That's kept everything in perspective."

"Except when it comes to shoes." A sparkle in his eyes said he was teasing, but he set down his sandwich and signaled her to stretch out her leg. "C'mon, let's see 'em."

She waited for a few patrons to shuffle past then showed off a Giuseppe Zanotti cork-heeled stiletto. The shoes were a pop of summertime glam to complement her tailored jacket and short pleated skirt. "Boss, women have a special relationship with footwear. Don't judge, just accept it."

Grunting as if to say "Oh, bother," he took another bite of the sub and it protruded out of his cheek as he said, "I give it a year before you convert one of your rooms into a shoe museum. I should lay money on that."

"Do as you please," she said flippantly, "but you'll lose." Though she had thought about reorganizing her master closet to accommodate the collection, which was growing exponentially. A well-crafted, stylish pair of shoes had a way of hogging the attention from her more complicated accessory, which was hooked onto the back of her chair. "Anyway, you make me sound like that nursery rhyme about the old lady. No judging, remember?"

"I never agreed to that." Ozzie waved a napkin. "But I surrender. So you had a sleepover at Desert Luck Center. Turn up anything?"

"No, though I sensed the Blues were hoping I'd have something they could use. The guy they singled out, TreShawn Dibbs? He's got walls up."

Even so, there was a sweet sincerity about him.

"Otherwise, how was camp?"

"Hmm, positive, from my point of view, at any rate. High tension, a lot going on, dozens and dozens of personalities clashing." She waited while he had the waitress bring out a slice of cheesecake and a glass of mint water. "I certainly have more respect for Charlotte after being in such a concentrated area with those men."

Charlotte would appreciate that, but even more so an explanation of how Joey could point Zaf out as the man who shot her and not go ballistic that he turned out to be her blind date. She preferred to shelter this facet of her world from her friends, but sometimes messy truths escaped, anyway.

"Desert Luck's practically a town of its own," Ozzie commented.

"Still makes for close quarters. The men—their bodies *and* their egos—have a way of taking up space."

"They treating you right over there?"

"It's fine," she maintained. "Some don't want me around and others want me around for all the dirty reasons. But alas, my virtue's still intact."

He smirked.

"So is ODC missing me, or what?" Then she started in on the dessert.

"Of course we're missing you—and the daily supply of sweets." Joey stress-baked, finding it a nice way to relax and rediscover the feeling of being a young girl buzzing around the kitchen, creating treats that her parents would sell at the flower shop.

"Folks got used to that first-thing-in-the-morning sugar rush. I might get boycotted for letting the Blues steal you away."

She almost beamed and flipped to sentimental mode, but her supervisor never knew what to do with emotional women. He liked to say that was the reason his wife filed for divorce a few years back, though it was a poorly veiled secret that the woman had moved on to a wealthier man.

"Next time I whip something up, I'll drop off the surplus—though I do like the idea of being missed. It's nice, says y'all care."

"Of course we care. We like— We're glad you—" Ozzie crumpled his napkin, visibly uncomfortable with the awkwardness of reassuring a colleague that she wasn't so bad to have around, after all. "You're okay, Joey. Everyone agrees. Things ought to be back to normal once you come back."

"Thanks, boss."

"Ah, jeez, don't act like I gave you a compliment or something. Last thing I need is for that to be going around."

"Breaking news. Ozzie Salvinski actually gives two beans about his coworkers." She nibbled the end of her fork, enjoying the withering look that earned her. "Fine, I'll stop now."

"Yeah, you'll have to." He pointed to his wristwatch. "Gotta head back to the office."

"Ozzie, quickly, before you go." Joey knuckled her dessert plate aside, slanted forward. "If I need to be hooked up—search warrant, surveillance, forensics, maybe—can I depend on you?"

"You planning on pulling something out of the trick bag for the Slayers?" he asked quietly, brows knit tightly.

"Hypothetically, okay, sure."

"Joey, what the hell's going on?"

I think a war's been started and I need to know what my options are. "I might need protection. Can't get into specifics, mainly because I don't have them. But it's just… just a feeling, I suppose."

"Do Marshall and Tem know about this?"

"No. It's trouble they don't need. If you can keep the lid on this, that'd be helpful."

"All right."

"So can I depend on you?"

"I'll do what I can, Joey. Don't forget the means of protection you already have."

Meaning her weapon. She didn't want more bloody violence in her memory, hadn't resorted to deadly force since before her move to Nevada. "I'm talking to you because I don't want it to come to that."

He nodded but looked skeptical. "You're ex-DEA, were chummy with ICE… Your network's more elite, so you're probably barking up the wrong tree. But whatever I can do, Joey, I will."

Left alone, Joey picked at the half-eaten cheesecake. Her network *was* more elite—far more elite than Ozzie suspected. Only, she refused to tap every resource within reach.

Even so, Gian DiGorgio wouldn't drop his grudge against her simply because he was served a boilerplate restraining order.

DiGorgio isn't some playground bully.

She swallowed down some mint water, but still felt as though a brick was lodged in her throat. Dragging in a breath, she looked out the window. The Ferrari waited in its darkly seductive magnificence, yet she wondered if lurking in every crevice on the street was somebody who'd been paid to harm her.

Damn Zaf. Damn him for coming back to her now. Damn him for forcing her to face this.

And damn him for being the most cunning and well-connected man she knew.

Joey took out her phone. She wasn't sure that the contact number her "blind date" had provided was still a viable way to reach him, but she had to give it a try.

"Jo?"

What did it mean that his voice could flood her senses? What did it even mean that she wanted him, flesh to flesh, yet hated the Machiavellian part of his personality that surfaced as some sort of wicked alter ego?

"It's me," she said, looking across at the people in the café, though not really seeing any of them. "About last night."

"What you did—I deserved that. I pushed you too far," Zaf apologized. "It's got to be overwhelming as all hell."

"It wouldn't be if it were someone else. But it's *me*, Zaf." And she was frightened.

"When you're ready to deal with this, call me. I still have the light beer."

She had to smile at that. "Can you get to the Strip? I'm at a side-street café. Nickel's."

He paused. Then, "I don't want to chase you, Jo."

"No chase. No tricks. I'll be here."

Almost fifteen minutes later Joey saw him emerge from a deep gray pickup truck that she was certain she'd seen scale rocky terrain on a television ad.

Attraction made her heart hurt. That crisp button-down he'd roughened up by rolling the sleeves and opening the collar was too perfectly made for his tight muscles. The belt snaked around his hips called too much attention to the region of his body she'd touched with authority yesterday in the library.

The open-carry holster at his waistband reminded her of who they were and where they'd come from.

As he tucked his keys into his pocket, she saw a bulky watch, onyx beads and a pair of thin leather straps wrapped around one wrist.

Dios. Te dessio.

As if he'd heard her thoughts, Zaf looked at her through the window. She raised her hand, flattened the palm against the glass.

She could perceive nothing from his expression, and put down her hand before he entered Nickel's and sought her table in that casual, unhurried way that threatened to make her smile.

"How you holding up?" he asked, lowering onto the vacant chair. "I left you with a lot to deal with yesterday."

"And I'm dealing with it. Kind of." She propped her elbows on the table, cupped her chin with both hands. "Were you worried about me, when you got to the house?"

"At first. Then, when I realized you were too smart to react carelessly and were sending me a message, I was pissed. Then I was proud of you for bringing me down a notch."

"We were always big on give and take, weren't we, Zaf?"

"Yeah." He reached for her hand, brought it to him. By the time she noticed the mocha-colored smear of dessert topping on her knuckle, he'd already taken it away with a warm, openmouthed kiss. "What was that?"

"Irish cream cheesecake. I'd offer you some, but I massacred it."

"Next time."

Next time, as though they were lovers and had the luxury of moments like this that weren't underscored with emotional upheaval.

"So what did you bring, Zaf?"

"Sam Adams and information. Both in my truck." He shot a glance out the window. "Where's your Chevy?"

"At home. I'm driving the black Ferrari."

"Ferrari?"

"Courtesy of Marshall and Tem Blue. I'm borrowing it while I do a job for them in Mount Charleston."

"You're working for them? One of DiGorgio's godsons is in talks with the team, Jo."

She'd heard Nate's brother was meeting with the Slayers about a coaching position. The Blues' hiring processes were baffling to front office outsiders, but their system obviously worked. They'd taken a losing franchise and turned it into championship-winning gold.

"It was my decision." She didn't clarify that the Blues and her supervisor had been particularly crafty about getting her to consider.

"I want you to be careful."

She reclaimed her hand because it'd be easier to concentrate if she wasn't preoccupied with urges to work her fingers into his dangerous mouth or yank free the rest of the buttons on his shirt. "How did you think this whole 'protecting Joey' plan was going to work?"

"Get close. Be a temporary fixture in your life. Since you're single now—"

"Are you?" she blurted. *Way to go there, slick.*

"Single? Yeah. I can't do to someone else what I did to you, Jo."

"It gets lonely. Sometimes."

He didn't agree, or admit that sometimes he was lonely, too, and that left her feeling at some strange, vulnerable disadvantage.

"Since I broke up with my last boyfriend, I mean. Things were good with Parker."

"Yet you went to a dating expert to find someone new." There was no blatant hostility in his words, but she felt hotter in the face, anyway.

"Just a way to occupy the lonely nights. Plus, I was hoping for someone who'd stick around to be my date for my friend Charlotte's wedding."

"So Romeo and Juliet end up with a happy ending, after all," he said quietly. "The wedding's next month."

She also thought of Nate and Charlotte as Shakespeare's star-crossed lovers. How could it be that after so much time apart, so much destruction between them, she and Zaf were still in sync with each other? "You know a lot about it. Keeping up with the society pages?"

"Research. What you said before—I can do that for you."

"You'd be my wedding date?"

"I'll do that for you, Jo." The seriousness, the unhidden want, acted as a magnet, pulling her hand across the table again until her pale fingers were stroking along the veins on his arm. "I'll stick around. I'll occupy the lonely nights. Let me protect you."

Oh. My. God. An emotionally tortured secret agent taking up the role of boyfriend to shield her from a sadistic crook? This didn't qualify as the daily happenings of an average small-town girl from Texas. Except, she *wasn't* an average small-town girl. She'd lost that part of herself.

"I can't do this, Zaf," she said, withdrawing her hand and standing up. "I can't give you an answer on the spot. Let's walk."

He joined her outside but once they turned onto the Strip, they lost all illusions of privacy. People—from giddy tourists to bored-looking locals to eager street entertainers—were all enmeshed.

"What's a man got to do to get you all to himself?"

Joey jabbed her cane down, stopping, letting sidewalk traffic coast around her. She stared at Zaf, watching him move easily with the crowd, completely unaware that she was no longer at his side. As pissed as she was at his bold question, she was amused that she could give him the slip. If she wanted to, she could disappear again and let him spend another sweltering Sin City night trying to track her down.

Several feet ahead, he did a double take, and folks shoved past him then edged out of his way as he cut through the stream of passersby until he was directly in front of her.

"Josephine, what the hell was that?"

Joey slid the end of her cane on the sidewalk in front of her. "Don't cross this line, Zaf. If you do, you'll be in my personal space and I won't like you much. If it helps, I got a great look at your butt. It's a nice butt."

He drilled his fingers through his dark hair, wrecking his *GQ* millionaire look. Actually, the unbuttoned collar had done that. And the heat he was packing in his holster. And, yeah, that edge about him that had nothing to do with boardrooms and everything to do with hunting a threat.

A threat targeted at *her*.

"Jo," he pleaded quietly, and she slid her cane back a few inches. "I'm here to protect you. How can I prove that?"

"One question at a time," she said. The cane retreated a few inches more, and then it was at her side, and she was letting him into her personal space. "You want to know what a man has to do to get me to himself?"

"We need privacy if we're going to agree on a plan. A sidewalk on the Strip doesn't say privacy to me."

"What does, then?" She watched him cross her invisible border, was suddenly and irrationally impatient for him to touch her the way he had before the violence had separated them. "Your hotel suite?"

"We could go with that, Jo. Nothing says privacy more than a Do Not Disturb sign on the doorknob." Zaf leaned forward, knocking back her curls from her face. "But I've got something else in mind."

"What?" They began their trek back to the street that held their vehicles.

"Invite me into your house. I want to sweep for bugs, tighten up the security. But I won't cross that line unless you ask me to."

"So we *have* changed, haven't we?" She stopped, but this time didn't let him leave her. "You used to know what I wanted without me needing to ask."

"I can't take risks when it comes to you. I've made mistakes. I've been wrong before—hurt you before."

"Archangel made me a victim," she said pointedly. She had to do this, dredge up how his clouded judgment had failed them both. Who stood so close to her this moment? Zaf, the man who could laugh at a joke and fill her up with joy? Or Archangel, the messenger, the black-ops genius with a vendetta to settle?

"I'm not him," Zaf said. "I'm not the other guy. You need to know that I wasn't really in league with that group. I wasn't going to move drugs for them, but they had to think I was on their side because they were going to lead me to the sons of bitches who killed Raphael."

Raphael, his younger cousin from Pakistan who'd been murdered during a trip to the US.

"You didn't turn? But no one told me it was a cover."

"Only our team leader knew, Jo. It had to be that way."

"You didn't trust me with your plan…"

He hadn't trusted her, then she hadn't trusted him, and devastation had wound up touching them both.

"I messed up," he said with regret. "Lying to you. Firing that weapon. I didn't want to come back and reopen the wounds. I swear to you, I didn't want this for you."

But here he was, in spite of himself.

"What about what *I* want, Zaf?" Did he know? Did it even matter to him? She couldn't find the words to guide him, but she ached, standing there unfulfilled and torn to pieces inside.

"I'm sorry. I'm so sorry, Jo." The words grabbed her, yanked her closer until she was curling an arm around his waist. His mouth descended on hers. She didn't care that they were on the street, in the way and on display for the mass of folks shopping and jogging and hurrying along.

Someone bumped them and they parted.

Breathing hard, she stared at the tears collected in his eyes. There was a war inside him. Remorse versus lust. "I believe you," she told him. She wanted this—proof that he cared.

"After what happened to you, I let go of the hunt."

Then he'd let go of Archangel, too, and was only Zaf.

Joey kissed him—that sullen mouth, that lean bristly bearded jaw, his tears. Arousal made her limbs too heavy, but she couldn't care about that when he lifted her just enough to transport her out of the middle of the sidewalk.

The robust sound of accordions and some indiscernible wind instruments grew louder as he set her down. Polka music.

But she couldn't care about that, either.

If this moment with Zaf was what she could get, then she would take it.

The kiss was bruising and his hold too tight, however, she wanted to emerge on the other side of hurt because she couldn't let herself be a victim any longer. She was a survivor. She'd survived a bullet, lies and losing the man she loved.

He turned her to face the window. They were still on

the sidewalk, with cracked concrete under their feet, but in front of a store she was greedy for the semblance of seclusion.

The sun shone bright and she saw their reflection in the glass. They weren't the people they'd been five years ago. Now they were too guarded and too hungry for something the other possessed.

Neither of them in love.

This was about arousal. It was about need and it was about desire. But it wasn't love.

I can't care about that. I can't want that.

Joey heard the footsteps and voices of passersby, but she stood her ground, remained reflected in a storefront's glass with a hard man behind her.

If he paid attention, if he really tried, he'd know what she wanted.

Zaf's hand rose to her ear, tracing the shell as he leaned over her to take the lobe into his mouth. "After DiGorgio's dealt with, I'll stand back. I'll let you live your life in peace. Swear to God."

"Then this is all temporary?"

"It's—" he kissed her neck and she arched into his touch "—an early jump on occupying those lonely nights. You good with that?"

"Good." To demonstrate, she rested her cane against the store's brick facing and pressed her backside to the wall of his body.

Zaf held her around the waist with one strong arm, and the other hand moved down the front of her with unmistakable intent. "What you said yesterday—keep your word. Don't forgive me, Jo. And don't love me."

Yesterday when she'd touched him, pain and mixed-up feelings had prevailed over all else. Today she needed passion to be victorious.

Focusing on them and not on what or who was on the

other side of the window, Joey watched the muscles in his arm leap as his hand curved underneath her short skirt, and was only mildly aware of traffic and pedestrians and polka music.

Parting her legs, she gasped at the impression of his erection against her ass. Give and take was what they did. Giving, she pressed into him and got a hoarse moan in return. Taking, she accepted the invasion of his fingers beneath her thong.

He didn't test her with one before introducing the other—just twisted two in, withdrew, then went in deeper. Each thrust of his fingers inside her and brush of his palm to her clit was a shock to her entire anatomy.

I shouldn't watch, she chastised herself. But then, why not watch? They were Zaf and Joey again, together again, and it was a miracle.

Even if time and violence had irrevocably changed them.

Owning this, she looked at the glass. She was a horny, wild mess. And Zaf was just as horny, wild and messy.

Clutching the arm that supported her, she watched herself ride his fingers until an orgasm brought her up high then dropped her down fast.

Euphoria made Joey dizzy, drunk, but she owned that, too. Unable to apologize or feel shame, she could only catch her breath and wear a tremulous little smile as people who'd paused in rapt voyeurism now scattered and someone stomping across the sidewalk behind them condemned them: "People banging on the street. This is *exactly* why it's called Sin City!"

When Zaf let her go, she pulled him back for a kiss. Indulging, she sucked in the taste of his skin. It was too soon to say goodbye to this…to the one thing that had always been right between them. "Come home with me."

Chapter 6

"Your house smells like a party."

Zaf meant the words to cut away some of the tension in Joey's living room, but she hadn't heard him.

Or she was ignoring him.

Standing stock-still in the open foyer, her skin pale and her eyes angry, she'd retreated.

She wasn't the same woman who surrendered to him on an overcrowded street. The heat, the submission that had set his blood on simmer, was gone.

Now he was cold, and he was pissed off that while she was in his arms, an intruder was in her house. If he could roll reality back a couple of hours to when they were close, connected, damn it, he would.

Then he might have a chance in Hades of sparing her the shock of coming home to find her place so altered.

Nothing was missing, but she insisted so many small things had been touched—mail removed from the box on the curb and filed in the quirky little holder on the entryway table…the mismatched sofa pillows neatened…dishes retrieved from the dishwasher and stacked on the counter… a pile of lingerie transferred from the coffee table to a laundry basket.

It was a message sent, that the "top-rated" security company's decal and rudimentary configuration were as deterring as the welcome mat on the porch.

Zaf hadn't made matters better by asking the fatal question, "Are you sure this isn't how you left it?"

"When have I ever been known to organize my mail in alphabetical order?" she'd cried. "*Of course* I'm sure. And before you ask, no, I don't usually receive visits from obsessive-compulsive cleaning fairies."

"I just needed to be certain." *Before I pay that bastard DiGorgio a visit of my own.*

Then and there he would've staked his life that Gian DiGorgio, a tyrannical man as greedy for control as he was for money, had given Joey's home a personal touch. But when she'd moved into the next room and reemerged holding a piece of paper with a tissue, his gut instinct had been confirmed.

"I took my gun out of storage to clean it," she'd said. "This was sitting on top of the box."

A note, with two words written in careful print. "Be careful."

Taking off, Joey had burst past him and out the door, her cane stabbing the ground. He'd followed, taking no chances on leaving her alone, and had watched her cut across the lawn to a neighbor who'd been unbuckling a couple of jabbering children from an SUV.

"Aggie?" she'd asked. "Hey, did you notice anyone in front of my place today?"

The woman's gaze had stalled on him, taking a moment to strip him and get her fill, then she said, "The kids had activities all over the city, so I've been in and out of the house chauffeuring them around. Oh, but hang on." Aggie had sent her kids inside and continued. "They forgot their floaties for the pool, so we doubled back not too long ago. I saw a car idling across the street. Can't say how long it'd been there. It was black, very expensive-looking, kind of like the one in your driveway."

"Can you give me more details? Make? Model? License plate, maybe? What about the driver?"

"Well, no, none of that. I've never seen a car like that in my life. And on a single-mom income I didn't want to look too closely because I'd end up totally jelly that I can't afford it." Concern had crossed Aggie's face, but it had given way to something crackling and sexual as she looked to Zaf. "Seriously, I *cannot* express how frustrating it is to want something the second you see it, and know it can't be yours."

"If everyone can keep their eyes open—"

"Definitely. I'll email the POA and we'll get a neighborhood watch alert sent to the loop. Now that school's out, we need to be especially watchful." Aggie added cheerfully, "And when are we going to catch up, anyway, Joey? Looks like you're living the dream, with the sexy car and the even sexier guy."

Joey had seemed thrown off guard by the woman's comment. "Oh—the car's something I'm trying out, and this is Zaf. We used to work together."

"Mmm. Guess you deserve the perks. I'm not tough enough to be a crime-fighter."

"You're a mom, Aggie. You're plenty tough."

And the women who took on the duties of both—they were damn tough. But he'd kept the thought to himself.

When he and Joey had returned to her house, he'd gotten a hold of a security specialist who owed him a solid and was able to disable the vulnerable system and install a wireless one.

Now they were alone and Joey refused to sit down or touch anything.

"It smells like sweets in here," he said, coming into the foyer and trying again to reach her to some degree. "Like a bakery."

"I bake." Finally, a response.

"Oh, yeah? You didn't when I knew you."

Joey had blanched further, as though tighter security had done absolutely nothing to restore her sense of safety. "There was quite a bit of downtime, with post-op and PT. I didn't want to take it easy, so I found something to keep me busy and help me handle stress." For the first time in several minutes, she moved. Standing in a tense position for so long must've stiffened her hip joint because a halting stride brought her into the kitchen. "The other night I made key-lime tartlets. It smells like I just pulled them from the oven."

"I would've guessed cake. Would've been wrong."

"Well." She went to the counter, reached for a stool but, as though DiGorgio was sitting on it, she drew back. "Well, maybe I'll make cake tonight. Yellow cake. Marshmallow buttercream frosting. That'd be good, right?"

"Cake tonight. Yeah, that'd be fine with me. If that's what you want?"

She shook her head. "When did it become about what I want?"

"Jo—"

"Zaf, I swear you don't want to discount what I'm saying right now. I can't remember the last time my life has been completely under my control. I obey and make concessions to please people, and when I don't, I feel guilty. DiGorgio has been in my house—my *home*, Zaf, my kitchen and my bedroom—and why? Because he wanted to run corruption in this city and I got in his way."

"He won't touch you."

"You can't promise me that. He's openly intimidating me."

"Want to call the cops, put something on record?"

"And report that someone came here, tidied up and left a *be careful* note on a strongbox where I keep my weapon? We have nothing concrete to attach this to DiGorgio. Our only witness is a person who loosely remembers seeing an expensive black car across the street. All that's going to be is paperwork the PD doesn't want to be bothered with."

"What about your cop, Parker?"

"I'd rather not plant any ideas in his head that I'm fabricating reasons to reel him back into my life. He's not my own personal protector. You are."

"You told your neighbor Aggie that we used to work together. I thought our story put us in a closer relationship than ex-coworkers."

Joey rubbed her eyes. "I was thrown off. Damn it, it's strange to call you my boyfriend."

"I don't remember you having difficulty taking on a cover before."

"This isn't just another assignment. It's the two of us pretending to be who we used to be. We were together for two years, but you and I haven't seen each other in five. In all that time, I have tried to forget we loved each other."

Tell the lie. Protect her. You're here to protect her, nothing more.

"Josephine…" *Say it. Say it to protect her.* "I didn't love you."

Hell, it burned to watch emptiness flood her eyes. But it had to be done. Love was like a baby's lullaby, soothing them as it weakened their instincts. He couldn't let it happen again. She wouldn't be tempted to believe they could recapture love if she thought they'd never had it to begin with.

"You said the words, Zaf. I heard them."

"When you were down. You were shot. Bleeding. I needed to keep you focused on something. I said what I did to engage you."

"But we were into each other. It felt real."

"It was sex. Friendship, too. But those things, they're not love. Have you loved every man you've slept with?"

"No. But I thought—"

A head shake interrupted her. "It wasn't what you thought. You're capable of that. I'm not."

Oh, God, he wished that were true. The damning truth was he might've loved her from the second he met her in Mexico, and it had taken time for him to let himself realize it. He cursed himself for not leaving her in the past where she belonged, but right now, in her kitchen with lies and screwups tugging them apart, he loved her.

As she glowered at him as if he was the vilest bastard to have ever walked this earth, he was sure she wouldn't form some attachment that might be impossible to break when the time came for him to walk out of her life again.

Because, as much as it seared the place inside him that should've housed his heart, he couldn't stay.

"You cared about me, Zaf," she persisted.

"Yeah. As a friend, somebody on my unit, somebody I liked having in my bed."

"Great talk, then," she said crisply. "This place is too quiet. A man gets access to my house and now it's a tomb? No, not okay. I'm putting the TV on."

He knew she was storing the hurt away. She would process it later and there would be tears. He hated being the reason for them.

Noise swirled through the air but didn't overtake the friction. She came back into the kitchen with the Samuel Adams Light he'd brought in from his truck.

It was the beer he carted to her door last night, intending to sweep the premises and hash out a plan, but she'd evaded him, and DiGorgio had gained entry before Zaf could find her again.

Trust was an integral component of a mission. They both knew it. Love complicated things and made them careless.

"Dios." Joey yanked on a card that had been pinned to the refrigerator with a sunflower magnet.

"What is it?"

"It's from my parents. An invitation to the Esposito *and* de la Peña family reunion." She opened the card, kissed it and closed it.

"Sounds like a big deal."

"It is. Their parties are legendary. My parents' families were rivals, believe it or not. When my mother and father got married, the bad blood started to go away. Thirty-six years later and they're hosting family reunions together." She set the invitation on the counter and reached for a packet of Jelly Belly. "I'm not going, but it's a beautiful card."

Zaf's hand ventured forward, and when she didn't slap it away he picked up the invitation. Second week of August at the Yellow Hawk Ranch in June Creek, Texas.

Chewing the candy, she spied him quietly. Then, "If DiGorgio or one of his men were in this room, stacking dishes on this counter, then they probably saw the invitation. And I'm mad as hell about it."

"Call your parents. Warn them to be vigilant."

Not that they exactly needed the warning. They were nothing if not vigilant…

"They're going to go crazy worrying. Mamá will insist that I come down to Texas where I'll be safe with the family. That's her way. And then Papá will agree with her and I'll lose my mind."

"It's what you do for family," he said. "They'll do what's necessary to protect you, Jo."

"Don't I know it," she said on a sigh.

Her family was not a typical hovering group. Anita Esposito de la Peña wasn't an ordinary mother hen.

But to reveal to Joey what he knew would be not just counterproductive; it'd obliterate what he'd come to Las Vegas to accomplish.

"You remind me of them—of the family," she said thoughtfully. "Maybe that's why I got hooked on you the way I did. Y'all have that 'family first, family only' mentality."

He had thought Joey didn't understand his quest to find the drug lord who'd held his cousin prisoner before murdering him. Ransoms had been paid, press conferences held, pleas for mercy broadcast across nations, but ultimately a young man who believed in the good in folks had lost his life.

Zaf had failed Raphael, a college-bound Pakistani kid on track to become an environmental activist. During Raphael's trip to the States, Zaf had been responsible for him but had accepted an undercover assignment midway through Raphael's stay. He'd felt uneasy about leaving the kid.

"I'm sending you up to Jersey, Raphael. Mom and Dad will keep your ass out of trouble."

"No, let me stay in Washington. It makes sense. I'm going to college here. I'm going to work here, too."

While Zaf was gone, his cousin had joined a counterterrorism group and ended up a target then a victim.

From the moment Zaf had found out, he'd been on a hunt. He wanted to find the killer, isolate him and confront him face-to-face. He wanted to see justice firsthand—hand it down himself.

Today he'd told Joey he had given up the vendetta. But that had been a lie in exchange for her trust.

With trust came cooperation, and he needed both to keep her safe.

"You don't particularly like that detail about me," he said to her, sitting on a stool.

"Zaf, your cousin's death ate you alive. It distorted your thinking. You hid it well when we were first together, but eventually everything you did was motivated by some master plan to avenge him. I was hurt because of it."

He wanted to avenge that, too. Which was why he couldn't give up now.

"Do you know how Raphael was killed? What they did to him?"

She relented, her face pinched with pain. "I was informed."

Nodding, he twisted the silver ring on his middle finger. It was Raphael's, left behind the day he'd been abducted. Zaf's aunt had insisted he keep it. She'd never blamed him, but he blamed himself.

Suddenly, Joey left the room. When she came back she was holding a key. "The spare from your badass locksmith."

"Asking me to stay?"

"It's the practical way to do this. People might wonder why my boyfriend's shacking up in some undisclosed hotel room. There's a guest room and a hall bath. The master bedroom's my sanctuary…but since some creeper did a walk-through today, that's a moot point."

"I'm not here to invade your privacy. If I can stay out of your way, I will."

"Fair enough."

"How do you suggest I earn my keep?"

She grinned impishly. "How about using your handyman skills to build me a shoe museum?"

"A what?"

"Shoe closet. A sanctuary for my footwear. I have a lot."

"Kind of odd request, but if you want it—"

"No, forget it. I was being silly."

"I'm going to do it. For real."

Releasing his gun and emptying his pocket, he set everything on the counter. Phone, untraceable phone, wallet, money clip, cigarettes, key ring—

"Whoa, whoa and whoa. I'm not a hard-ass by any means, but *that's* a no-no in my home." Joey was pointing to the cigarettes. "You never smoked."

"What baking does for you, smoking does for me—fills the downtime and eases the stress."

"Are we at an impasse? Suppose I want to kiss you? I don't want to taste cigarettes."

"You thinking about kissing me?"

"Um, no." Joey's rosy cheeks contradicted her words. "Eventually, we *will* kiss again. If we're going forward with this boyfriend-girlfriend ruse, it ought to look authentic."

Zaf beckoned her to him, turning away from the counter to give her room to get close. Cupping her head, he brought her face to his and kissed her.

The taste of jelly beans flooded his tongue and he smiled against her mouth. "So how was that?"

"Really good. It's been a while since anyone's kissed me the way you do."

"What about that cop of yours?"

"He's an exceptional kisser and sometimes I miss that about him. But the relationship soured."

"What'd he do?"

"Fell in love with me."

Zaf held himself still, searching her eyes. "Then what did *you* do?"

"Unlike you, Zaf," she said, "I can't tell someone I love them if I don't mean it. It was nice to have somebody, but Parker was ready to move forward and apparently, in some ways I'm stuck where you left me five years ago."

He took his hand from her hair, lightly gripped the front of her jacket and urged her closer.

I lied, he almost whispered. *I love you and am paying hell for it.*

Slowly, he bent toward her until his head rested against her chest and he could feel her fingers weaving through his hair. "If I had it in me to love anybody, it'd be you, Josephine."

"No consolation prize necessary."

"I'm sorry."

"Don't mention it." She disentangled herself. "I need to step away from this for a bit, okay? I promised Charlotte a gabfest, so I'm going to see if she's free for a night out."

"I'm going with you."

"Girls' night means no men allowed. I need normalcy, Zaf, for a little while."

"You're skipping out on me knowing your next-door neighbor's in heat?"

"Aggie's not in heat."

"She eye-fucked me."

"She eye-fucks everyone. Don't be so sensitive." She frowned a little. "Are you thinking about getting some of my neighbor's sugar?"

"No, I'm not. Aggie's a beautiful woman. The thing is, you're also a beautiful woman and we have this deal going. I intend to hold up my end of it."

"Letting you be the man to keep me company through the lonely nights… That's for show, though."

"It doesn't all have to be." He would go out tonight, but not for a shallow hookup. Since he didn't intend to give up the room he'd been renting for the past few months, he would collect some items to keep on site in her house.

Living with Joey, loving her, yet not being with her would be a challenge and retribution.

"Go out with your friend, clear your head." *Then come back to me.*

Zaf shut the thought down. He watched her go then hunkered down to strategize an in-person visit with Gian DiGorgio. Trespassing on Joey's property was a personal attack, and Zaf would confront that bastard personally. As he was mapping out a contacts web, she popped into the doorway.

"Meeting Lottie on the Strip," she said, but he hardly heard her.

The strapless silk dress was body paint with a side zip, and her hair had been teased into some style that could probably best be called after-sex. The leather walking stick and superskinny high heels gave her an edgy, hard rock "look, don't touch" vibe.

"Christ, Joey…"

"What's the matter?" she asked softly. "You look as if you don't want to let me go."

But he had to. Archangel was his destiny, who he was meant to be, and she didn't deserve the danger that came with him. "Call me if you need me."

"Oh. Then…" She hesitated, and he wished she wouldn't give him ample time to lose his wits, walk over and kiss the hell out of her. "Good night."

When she left, stress threatened to fetter him. A few days ago he wouldn't have thought twice about reaching for a cigarette. But he wanted the taste of her kiss.

Settling for a substitute, he unrolled her half-empty packet of jelly beans. Tomorrow he'd replace them. All he had to do was get through tonight.

"As your maid of honor," Joey proclaimed, shot glass in hand as the Hyde Bellagio ruckus pulsed in her ears, "my first order of rabble-rousing is to host a wicked bridal shower that will scandalize Tem."

Across their fountain-view table, Charlotte threw her head back and laughed. The sequins on her tank top shimmered but were hilariously lackluster compared to the vibrant brilliance of the diamond decorating her hand. The woman was wearing 1.5 million dollars of sparkling fire on her finger. "That party's going to get me disowned."

"Only if done right."

"I'm glad you decided to be in the wedding," her friend said after swallowing down the single-malt whiskey. She signaled for another, which their VIP host delivered promptly in a fresh glass with a linen napkin. "Are you having a second?"

"This *is* my second," Joey said, giggling. Charlotte was on her fourth and had what Joey estimated to be forty grand worth of whiskey in her system. From über-pricey liquor to complimentary bottle service for their table, they were enjoying the Blue experience. Charlotte's parents weren't only elite, they were supremely generous tippers. As such, the city's most glamorous venues adored them. "It'll have to be my last of the night. I drove here, in your father's novelty car."

"The Ferrari. Martha might feel slighted about that. She wanted to borrow it when he first acquired it, and his answer was a resounding Marshall Blue no."

"Maybe he didn't want his baby girl to be spoiled."

Charlotte and Joey both fell silent then laughed at the irony in that. Charlotte's much younger sister had not even a year ago been splashed across tabloids for her hard-partying exploits. Something remarkable had happened to Martha, though. She'd fallen in love. Now she was blazing up the corporate ladder within the Slayers' franchise, adopting a teenager, modeling an adorable baby bump, and—as of two weeks ago in an intimate beach ceremony—married to Joaquin Ryder, a champion prizefighter.

While Charlotte had only tossed around the idea of elop-ing, Martha and her man had gotten it done.

It was amazing to reflect on how drastically each of the Blue sisters' lives had blossomed this past year. The love bug had kissed them all, and Joey, who was as close as family but still on the outside, watched it unfold. While they could open their hearts to men who loved them, she couldn't take the risk. Clearly, she was immune to the love bug.

Oh, and the man she *did* love once hadn't loved her at all. It was the story of her life and she didn't appreciate it all that much.

"Sure you don't want more whiskey?" Charlotte checked. "You're staring into your empty glass. My driver won't mind dropping you at your place and we'll have the Ferrari sent over."

A first-class Hummer limo drop-off would be a tad much. Her neighborhood had already been subjected to too many unusual occurrences today.

"No, thanks, though it'd be lovely. Save it for next girls' night."

"All right. And since this *is* girls' night and our oppor-tunity to catch up on each other's lives—" Charlotte set down her glass and suddenly there was no trace of her li-quor buzz "—please tell me what's going on. I'm worried."

"What's going on, hmm? A lot, actually." A shift of her eyebrows and Charlotte took the hint to send off the host and server lingering nearby. "Gian DiGorgio, or one of his people, was in my house—uninvited, obviously—while I was at Desert Luck this morning."

"Gian DiGorgio," she repeated as the name and the meaning behind it registered. "He broke into your house? Wh-what…"

"I took too close of a look at him last summer. It was my duty to report what I found. The FBI, IRS, the Nevada

Gaming Commission—they had to be made aware. I'll never regret that I did the right thing."

"You started digging because you were concerned about who I was getting mixed up with. Nate and I, our relationship, set this in motion?"

"None of this is your fault. I'm glad it was discovered. DiGorgio and Nate's dad were *fixing football games*, for crying out loud. Ordering bounties, paying off players, the illegal gambling itself? Come on, that's serious."

"Gian should be in prison. Nate and his brother will never get past what he's done. And to think he's a free man after all of that?"

"He's a free man because he has more money and influence than you or even his godsons realize."

"So you do the right thing, act with integrity, and you're saddled with the fallout?"

"It happens, Lottie. I've seen this in my world. It's not pleasant, but the screwed-up reality is money defies everything."

"This is insane."

"Agreed. I assume I can kiss goodbye the hope of being invited to the Titanium Club in his casino," she quipped, because if she didn't joke she'd break apart.

"Joey, he's a sociopathic bastard and he won't get away with scaring you. Let me call my folks—"

"Put it down," Joey interrupted when Charlotte went for her phone. "Don't involve Marshall and Tem. This is the exact brand of drama they want to dodge."

"But you need someone to protect you."

"I have someone." Zaf didn't love her—*had never* loved her—but he was making real efforts to ensure her safety. She was adult enough to accept their circumstances for what they were. "The blind date from the library. He's also my wedding date, FYI."

"Is this one of your sarcastic jokes?"

"No."

"In the gallery you said he's the guy who shot you, then you said, 'Oh, it's complicated' and shooed me out of there. Now he's your date to my wedding?"

"And he's living with me. And I'm crazy attracted to him."

"And you *must* be joking. This cannot be an actual, serious conversation."

Joey sighed, but not out of frustration. Charlotte and Aggie and every other friend who'd crept into Joey's life after she'd moved to Las Vegas to begin again as a civilian—they had innocence about them that she envied. They didn't have an intimate relationship with society's underbelly, didn't know what it was to use deception, manipulation and sometimes violence as tools to seek a greater good.

She didn't speak about the horrors she saw or the devastation she experienced. It was why Charlotte—her closest friend—didn't know Joey had loved Zafir Ahmadi before he'd unintentionally shot her in an attempt to rescue her.

"Zaf was in black ops," Joey began carefully. "He and I hooked up during a case in Mexico seven years ago. We were hot and heavy for two years. I loved him. I began and ended with the man."

"He *shot* you, Joey."

"This is difficult to talk about, okay, Lottie? I need you to listen. Please." Charlotte looked ready to protest, but nodded and Joey continued. "Our unit was working a narcotics bust in Arizona five years ago. We were in a parking garage and it was so friggin' hot, so hard to breathe. Something felt off the entire time, and then it came out that Zaf had a deal going with the suspects. In exchange for some information of personal interest to him, he'd facilitate their drug deal and help them make a smooth escape. To know that the man I loved had turned dirty? It was gut-wrenching."

Charlotte sat, not blinking, her fist pressed to her heart, her head shaking slowly.

"It was a cover, though. I hadn't been made aware and I panicked. Someone grabbed me, was going to kill me. Zaf was trying to free me, but I didn't trust him. I couldn't trust him.

"He signaled to me that he'd fire his weapon, but when he was on the trigger I started kicking…and I was hit. The bullet went in through my abdomen, did some unpleasant things to my hip, and I've been angry for a long time."

"You thought he did it deliberately?"

"At first," she admitted. "It seemed implausible that it was a close-range mistake. He's a phenomenal sharp-shooter. And he's a brainiac, though not as bookish as your hot Joe College."

Charlotte's smile was sad. "Joey, this is heartbreaking."

"It's not meant to be. It's only the truth. I wanted the rage. I wanted to hate Zaf. But there were investigations and he'd fired for the right reasons. I wouldn't be here now if he hadn't. The trust between us was lost and as a result errors were made."

"When did you find out about the cover?"

"Today. Until today I thought he was an agent who lost his way but tried to be a hero in the end. The Bureau's seen it before."

"Now he's back. Why?"

"He found out Gian DiGorgio has been keeping an eye on me and he wants to put an end to it. This way he can be my bodyguard without alerting everyone around me, particularly your parents, that I need a bodyguard. We're handling this, so that's why you can't involve more people. Don't mention this to Marshall and Tem."

"What about Nate?"

"Not him, either. Besides, he's got plenty of complications with the whole Santino and Bindi thing." Nate's brother was apparently heart-and-soul in love with their father's much younger ex-fiancée—and tabloids were still enjoying the irony of it all.

"I can't lie to my fiancé."

A lie-free relationship? Joey thought such a thing was as real as a unicorn or a pot of gold at the end of a rainbow. "I can respect that. Should Nate ask you specifically if his godfather is stalking me, you have my blessing to tell him what you know."

"So this man…Zaf…he's living with you and watching your back?"

"We've agreed that he'll pretend to be my boyfriend until the DiGorgio problem has been solved."

"You said you're still attracted to him. How long before you start wanting *pretend* to become the real thing?"

"It's not like that, Lottie."

"You loved him once."

"Yeah, but as I also learned today, he didn't love me. He can't love, he claims. And I won't push."

"Jo," Charlotte said on a sigh, "this is by far the saddest girls' night out ever."

"Yeah," Joey murmured, and pointed outside, "and here's the rain for further emphasis." It seemed to complement the mood of the day, but having grown up on a ranch and surrounded by flowers, she appreciated rain. It'd been too long since she let herself get caught in it.

Charlotte picked up her phone. "Weather alert. Thunderstorm. Maybe now this heat and humidity will let up. Hope everyone's slowing their speed and watching out for downed power lines." They left the table for a view of lightning branching above the glittering city. "Would you think less of me if I left? I know it's early as heck, but I just want to put my arms around Nate and wait this storm out."

"That sounds disgustingly romantic." Joey gave her a one-armed hug. "Get out of here. Go be in love."

After Charlotte's driver collected her from the Bellagio, Joey set a course for home. The girls' night gabfest had ended early, but it was for the better. She still had plenty of time to pour her stress into a cake-baking session. Thank God, too, because she had plenty of stress. Talking about Zaf had left her on an emotional spin cycle.

I'm crazy attracted to him.

Had that been a lie? Was it only attraction?

Attraction hadn't compelled her to open her body to him on a crowded street. It didn't torment her with hunger for his touch and thirst for his taste. It didn't influence her to resent every day they'd been apart. It sure as hell didn't tempt her to forgive their mistakes and forget that no, he hadn't loved her.

Damn it, she needed it to be about attraction. About sex, really.

Turning onto her street, Joey found it completely dark under the bawling sky.

Power outage.

Did her heart rate kick up in fear that wasn't totally irrational? Yes. Did it give way to calmness the second she saw Zaf's truck in the driveway? Yes—and that disturbed her.

She'd never before minded being alone. Now that he was here, in her life and in her house on the darkest night of the summer, she was genuinely afraid to be without him.

"Not a good sign, *chica*," she warned herself, parking next to the truck and hurrying through the assaulting rain as quickly as her cane and stilettos would allow.

Muggy heat welcomed her home. The security system had a backup battery and she was relieved to find it still functioning unaffected. The same couldn't be said for the air conditioner. Was that worse than not being able to make a cake or having to remove her makeup without the aid of her electric magnifying mirror?

"Zaf," she called out, feeling around the dark for a route

to the kitchen drawer that held the candles. "A little light would've been awesome."

His voice came from the hall and a tiny golden glow preceded him. The light vanished then reappeared with a faint *snick*.

"Are you using a lighter?" she asked, then continued on to the kitchen.

"Correct. But not for cigarettes."

"You didn't smoke tonight?"

"Uh-uh. I ate the rest of your jelly beans." He paused and she couldn't tell where he was now. The guy had the stealth of a jungle predator. "I got a candle going in the bathroom. I was planning on lighting as many as I could find so you wouldn't stumble around in the dark."

"Oh. Thanks. Lottie and I cut girls' night short on account of the thunderstorm. The candles are in here."

"Where's here?"

"Kitchen."

She gathered tealights, votives and tapers. Providing the flame, he helped her place the candles in holders throughout the main rooms, and they separated to carry one to their respective bedrooms.

Dios, the house was hot. Before she got to her room, she put the holder on a hall table, lifted her hair off her neck and changed directions.

Backtracking, she wound up in front of the bathroom's open doorway and listened to the rush of water filling the tub.

Zaf opened the door wider. Candle flames flickered, offering leaping shadows across the walls. "Need something, Jo?"

Very much. "No. Are you gonna take a bath?"

"A dip. It's a hot night."

Stuck on pause, Joey watched him unfasten his belt. She

stood there, her hand in her hair, her skin sweltering inside a dress that was squeezing her tighter by the nanosecond.

"Hey, Joey, do you need something?" he asked again, yanking the belt free. The leather serpent hit the floor near his bare feet.

"No," she said again. She didn't *need* to continue to stand here; she wanted to.

"Uh… I'm about to get in that tub and I won't be doing it with my clothes on."

She couldn't move—couldn't manage to tell him to make her move. It was as if her mind refused to object to her body's decision to stay.

But Zaf didn't comment further. He turned, gracing her with a full frontal view as he stripped off the shirt.

Muscles constricted under tanned skin, taking hold of her complete attention. She dropped her hair and clutched her cane too fiercely, taking blatant inventory of the cut of his hip bones, the pattern of hair that arched up his abs and stretched across his chest.

A telling scar at the front of his shoulder had her coming a few steps closer. "That's a bullet wound. You were shot?"

"On a security job some months ago." The shirt joined the belt, and his hands gravitated to the front of his pants.

Arousal jumped inside her as fitfully as the shadows dancing up the walls.

He brought the pants down, kicked them off.

No underwear. Just him, standing in front of her in complete rugged nudity.

And here she thought she'd have a few seconds to brace herself or to perhaps reconsider and back away.

"Don't worry, this shouldn't last too much longer. The water's cold," he said, apparently noticing that she stared at his erection with openmouthed fascination.

Whoever had carved the design of this man's body evidently wanted to sink her with lust.

Zaf stood in front of the bathroom vanity and removed the silver ring. Her gaze tracked him from the vanity to the tub, and it hurt her to remember a time when she was at liberty to run her hand down the line of his spine and grasp his ass because his body belonged to her and hers belonged to him.

He turned the spigot. Lowering into the water, plowing his hands through and running them over his face and hair, he rested against the tub in a casual sprawl and considered her.

Beneath the nonchalance was taut intensity, danger that persuaded and provoked.

"Get in, Jo."

"There's a soaking tub in my bathroom." Or she could get in the car and blast the air. Or she could flee to any one of Vegas's downtown dens.

Staying here with Zaf wasn't her only option. But still she didn't move.

"Coming or going?" he asked.

"I don't know."

"Tell you what. Get a deck of cards."

Perplexed, she hesitated but the cavalier command was like a pat to her ass, urging her along. In the candlelit living room she found a catchall basket and dug up a box of Bicycle.

"Since you don't know and I'm not going to decide for you," he explained when she shook out the cards and handed them over, "let these figure it out."

She watched him shuffle with dexterity that had her mind drifting to other talents his hands were capable of.

"Higher card trumps. If it's yours, you walk. If it's mine, you get in with me. That sound fair?" When she nodded, he said, "Cut the cards. Lady first."

Joey took away the top half of the deck, revealing a ten of hearts. Not the best possibility, but a solid card.

Without a word, Zaf Charlier-cut the deck. Then, sitting back and taking a stab at a triumphant grin, he revealed the king of spades.

Chapter 7

"I'm not holding you to the game."

Joey was in the middle of wiggling the cards back into their box. Fumbling over her task, she dropped them. "There are clothes and cards on the floor, limited light, and you didn't put down a towel. This bathroom's a cautionary tale in the making."

This tub, in my arms, is a safe place for you.

She picked her way to the tub. "What do you mean, you're not holding me to the game?"

"Just what I said. If you leave this room, I won't follow in pursuit. The high card means nothing."

"Gallant of you, Zaf," she said, propping her cane against the tub. She bent and slipped off one shoe then held on to the tub's edge to remove the other. "But I take card playing seriously. When I cut the deck, I knew there was a fifty-fifty chance you'd get the high card."

"This isn't one other thing that's out of your control." Zaf felt the cords of his neck tighten and his blood rush to his penis—despite the scientific psychology of cold water's effect. "What you do next is your choice. But as a suggestion, take your dress off before you get in this tub. You *will* get wet."

"What a pervert. My mamá warned me about men like you."

"Your mamá's a smart cookie."

"She wouldn't want me to be alone with a brooding, mysterious fellow who *obviously* wants to do dirty things to me in a bathtub."

"So you have a choice to make."

"Mmm-hmm. You're here, I'm here and it's a lonely night, Zaf."

"That's all it can be about." *I'm a lying bastard. I love you and I'm too weak not to.*

"Just like when we cut those cards, I know what the stakes are."

He almost bowed up to gather her in his arms, but the stern determination on her face warded him off as if she'd snapped, "Don't interfere." She would come *to* him without his help.

He had the entire night to make her come *for* him.

Zaf widened his legs, creating space for her to settle when she gripped the edge of the tub and stepped in with her right foot first.

"Cold," she yelped. "It'll cool me down, but it's chillier than I expected. How are you coping?"

"My body decided to ignore it."

"I see that." Perched on the edge of the tub, running one foot over his under the water, she said, "This is as deep as I'm wading."

"Worried about what I might do, Jo?"

"Nope. Just assessing things." Thoughtfully, she reached out a palm and explored his bent knee. "Your body amazes me. The symmetry and the harshness... When we slept together, sometimes I woke up during the night and if I had trouble drifting off again, I would watch you sleep."

"I'm not the world's most peaceful sleeper." Night terrors sometimes ripped him from dreams and threw him out of bed in a cold sweat.

"I remember. Whenever I noticed you in an angry dream, I'd try to soothe you. God knows if it ever worked."

It had—often. Her gentle whispers and soothing touches had penetrated his subconscious, combating the demons that accessed him at his most vulnerable.

"Why stay in bed with a man fighting in his sleep and disturbing you?"

"I didn't want to leave you to suffer. I was thinking that in your sleep on some level you'd know you weren't alone. A girl in love—that was me." She took her hand away. As hot as it was in this room, he missed her warmth. "Men don't share my bed anymore. I'm a sprawler now."

"Sprawler?"

"Arms and legs spread. I spread out across the entire bed because it's all mine."

"What position are you in when you wake up?"

She was quiet and the house was quiet, and for a moment there was only the hammering rain and the toss of the wind. "Hugging a pillow." Discomfort had her posture straightening and her hands twisting the hem of her dress. "So what, anyway."

Water trailed down his body as he stood. Cupping her shoulders, he let the burst of desire expanding her pupils spellbind him. "The way your nipples pucker up and you watch me with your eyes half-closed like that when you're turned on… I swear that memory's chased me for five years. This night's gonna chase me for the rest of my days."

"No, it won't. When you do fall in love with somebody, you'll forget the little things about me."

"I told you I'm not capable of that."

"I think you are. It's going to be incredible. When you're in love and you embrace it, it's as if you're at this place that's the inverse of the worst you've ever felt. Joy can be as intense as misery. I've been there before, so I know."

She'd been there before with him. She'd loved him, a man who was undeserving and unable to put her first. She thought he'd given up being Archangel the vigilante hell-bent on righting a personal wrong, but that was a necessary lie. Zaf and Archangel were still two halves of the same man and he hadn't changed all that much.

Joey was the one who'd changed and sacrificed, and it wasn't fair. "I'm sorry, Jo."

"Don't do that—pity me. Don't touch me if you do pity me."

He touched her, pinching her supple bottom lip and swallowing down her gasping little moan in a kiss. "Something's telling me you want my touch no matter the reasons behind it. There's nothing wrong with wanting contact."

"Wait. Aggie and all sorts of uncomplicated women in this town would gift wrap their panties for you, yet you're in this stifling house doing bodyguard duty."

"And?"

"And I want to know if this attention and the kisses and the touching is all because you feel sorry for me."

Light and sound bloomed around them as the electricity was restored, but Joey didn't move. She waited for an answer. No, not *an* answer, but the one she wanted to hear.

Zaf emerged from the tub and walked naked out of the bathroom. The cold water hadn't cooled, calmed or numbed a damn thing between them.

The guest bedroom was too cheerful for his mood, with all the lamps now glowing along with the two votive candles Joey had given him. His duffel occupied a corner of the bed and he moved it to the floor. While Joey had been out with her friend, he'd brought clothes and equipment over from the bare-bones room he rented out of a dime-a-dozen motel.

It wasn't far past midnight, but he would yank on a pair of shorts and do a sprawl of his own across this bed. Maybe, if he didn't screw up and waste the night picturing Joey playing in the sheets and slithering around on the mattress, he would rest.

Detecting the tap of her cane nearby, he disregarded the common sense pleading with him to stay out of her way. He pursued the hallway, coming to an immediate, soundless stop when he saw her barefoot and beautiful, dousing a candle.

Joey lobbed a scowl at him. "What do *you* want?"

But the hostility didn't interrupt his stride. Taking the candle from her and plunking it on the table, he dipped a finger into the front of the silk bound across her breasts and jerked her to him.

"Come here."

"I'm here," she said.

"Closer."

She let the cane go. It slid free, clattering onto the wood floor, and she clung to his hips. Her fingers pressed into his damp flesh, and her russet eyes searched his with eager demand.

Zaf found her mouth wet and impatient. It invited him to the taste he couldn't resist, to a tongue that opened him and taunted with each deliberate stroke. Catching each of her lips between his teeth, he held on until she gave him a sexy little whimper. Pushing back her hair and winding it around his fist like a dark honey strap, he said, "This isn't pity, Jo. I don't pity-fuck."

They were rough words dressed up in even rougher tones, but this is how they were together from that first night in Mexico—blunt, natural, real.

Joey's hands rode up his body, at last linking behind his neck. He swung her up but paused to reach for the cane.

"Get it later," she tried to persuade. "It'll be a wet blanket on what we have going here."

"I'm not letting you feel trapped by leaving your stick out in the hall. You're free to get out of my bed and go whenever you want."

"Am I free to leave it here because it's a reminder of all kinds of unpleasant stuff that I don't want to wedge between us?"

"It's our reality. You need the damn thing, and I'm the reason for it. If that's too hard for us to face, then why are we doing this?"

"Leave it out here, the stick and all the hell." She kissed his chest, his Adam's apple. "I want contact. Give me that, okay?"

Contact. He could do that, because showing her more—such as the truth—would unleash trouble neither of them was meaning to tempt.

Swinging her up, he brought her to his room and set her in front of the bed. "Condoms, top middle dresser drawer," she said.

"You keep condoms in a guest room? Who do you let stay here?" Her soft, sweet laughter followed him as he took a couple. "About that dress you're wearing. If you'd followed my suggestion in the bathroom, you would already be out of it."

A naughty smile in place, Joey sought the side zipper. The zipper hissed as it slid down the track, parting her dress. The fabric surrendered, pooling onto the floor.

Chaste pink lace cradled her tits and draped over her pussy like a garnish on top of something he was dying to taste again.

Unkempt and writhing where she stood, Joey reached behind her to release her bra. He crouched to rid her of the panties, but halted when his eyes fastened on the darkened scar marring the peach-soft smooth skin on her abdomen.

She was so damn tough to withstand this world and survive his unforgivable mistakes. He couldn't help but love her. There would be no future with her, but he had himself to blame for that.

"Tell me if something hurts," he said, kissing her scar and curving his hand over her hip. "What can't you do?"

"Straddling you would be awkward."

"Awkward?"

"Okay, painful."

"What's good for you?"

"Missionary, if I hug you with my knees pulled up. Come inside me from behind…"

Zaf looked up at her. "Babe."

She laughed, shielding her eyes. "I was mad at you in the hall. Now I'm laughing."

They'd always had a way of provoking each other's highest highs and lowest lows. But he wanted to strip anger and humor away and discover what remained between them.

Still watching her, he pushed her panties down unceremoniously. He dragged the all-but-transparent fabric under his nostrils, then sucked on it before pitching it aside.

And the laughter died.

"I've missed you." Lying on the bed, she flipped onto her stomach. "Get on top of me. Cover me. That should feel nice for you."

Zaf wanted something beyond what would *feel nice* for him. He wanted her satisfied top to bottom, clean through.

Crawling onto the bed, knowing she was anticipating his mount, he changed direction and lay beside her.

Joey practically sprang up. The mattress barely shifted under her slight weight. It teased his self-control to not pin

her and catch one of those peaked nipples between his lips.
"Are we okay?"

"It's about you tonight. Control's what you want, isn't it?
So here is your opportunity. If you want control, take it."

"Zaf... I want *you*."

"Then take me."

Joey didn't want to lead.

How could he not know that? He *should* know.

She shook, impatient for reassurance that his body
wasn't deaf to the melody of hers, that he didn't have to
relearn her completely. But here he lay, choosing now of
all moments to relinquish control. Instead of setting the
tone, as he had out in the hall, he waited for her to act.

Was it really because she'd made an issue of not steering her own life—or was it because her fragility made
him skittish?

Zaf had never held back before, but he did now. It'd
been a while since she felt so damaged.

It's about contact. Only contact.

Reinforcing the steel protecting her heart, she touched
him. She began at his hairline, skimming her fingers over
the fine silken strands. Then she moved her knuckles down
the line of his whiskered jaw and ducked down to nuzzle it.

His coarse beard scratched; his chest hair tickled. Following the trail past his navel, she nestled between his
legs, twirled her fingers through his pubes then tugged.

Zaf's hips jerked and he reached down to clutch her
head. "What was *that* for?"

"Just making sure I have your attention."

"Damn it, you got it. Anything you want."

He was so weak for her. She wanted to bask in the
power, but could only focus on coaxing his pleasure.

Contact, she tried to remind herself, but it was next to

impossible to lie when high emotions weakened her resolution to keep this about just sex.

She missed handling him, watching his cock grow hard and heavy in her hand, feeling her mouth water for the first taste of him to sink into her tongue.

Sealing her lips over the tip, she hummed, grateful for the familiarity of this. Everything around them had changed, but this remained the same.

His hand moved from her head to the back of her neck. Spitting into her palm, she pumped his shaft. The wetter his flesh, the deeper she could take him. And the deeper she took him, the harder his fingers pressed into her. By morning there'd be impressions left behind.

On them both.

"Good you stopped there," he groaned when she let him slip free of her lips. "My turn."

"I'm in control, remember?" She pushed his chest and he lay flat on the bed again. "So here's what I'm doing with it."

Joey lowered again. The sides of her face were sore and her lips stung, but her mouth missed him. He was a jawbreaker of a man, but she gladly accepted the challenge.

Encouraging him to grind into her until she was able to tease his hair with her nose, she cupped his balls and swallowed. Coming up for air, she grinned and repeated the kiss.

The play of her muscles flexing around him had him crying out unfinished sentences and unintelligible words. Reluctantly, she let him go and massaged her throat.

Flopping on top of him, she let herself enjoy being the reason for his ragged breathing and the sweat on his skin.

"Jo. God, my Jo." He molded a hand to her ass, waking up her nerves with a squeeze and a slap. "Who taught you how to do that?"

"Do you really want me to answer that?"

"I'm trying to decide whether I should thank the guy or kill him."

"Then it doesn't matter. You and I—*we* matter." She couldn't hide her smile…couldn't hide that she was happy. But oddly, she was sad, too.

This intimacy wouldn't last. Even now, she was taking what she could get—not what she wanted. He wasn't capable of giving her that.

She had offered him love and he'd tied up her heart, preventing her from fathoming taking the risk with someone new. It had been bearable when she believed he loved her, too.

Knowing that he hadn't loved her and would never give her what she needed? *That* wasn't bearable.

But hey, didn't she always find a way to cope?

"Am I still in control?" she asked, searching his face for some sign that he could see through her pretenses and defenses. *You take over. Take me.*

"Get on your back."

Yes, sir. Hell, yes.

Joey dropped back into softness and opened herself. No, he hadn't said that was what he wanted, but her body knew. So did her heart.

"Everything about you is incredible," he said.

"*No soy perfecto.* You're seeing me through sex-tinted glasses."

"I didn't say perfect." He hesitated to raise her left leg higher but when he settled it over his shoulder, she didn't mind. "Some of the most incredible, beautiful things are flawed."

"Flawed. That, I am."

She felt his words on her inner thigh before he kissed her there. "This freckle? Incredible." He pinched her clit between two knuckles. "The way you squirm and moan when I do this? So incredible."

Then he added lips and introduced tongue, and she was flailing for something to cling to. This wasn't the antique-style iron bed in her room—there were no bars to clutch. The headboard behind the mountain of pillows was a solid mahogany slab, and her fingers slipped when they tried to gain purchase.

Nothing would help her ride out the sensations.

Bucking under him, she surrendered to a succession of moans, each louder than the one preceding it. His name belonged in her mouth, and his mouth belonged on her.

"Taste this," he commanded, sliding up her body. Kissing her, he tantalized her with lips slick from her own arousal. "I dreamed about this."

After he rolled a condom into place, she asked, "You've been dreaming about me, Zaf?"

He didn't answer her—not with words. Drawing up her knees, he thrust into her, spearing her, coming back to her in a way she hadn't believed was possible before finding him waiting for her in a library.

Zaf leaned until she could hug his shoulders. He'd given her something to hold on to. Watching his face as he moved inside her, she knew.

On some level that was deeper than friendship or sex, she'd gotten to him.

But, as they lay together with her weak leg draped over him and his hand on her scar, she said nothing.

Zaf was the first to speak. "I'm gonna get your cane now."

"Sending me on a walk of shame to my bedroom?" she murmured against his chest.

"No. There's no shame in this."

"I know. It was always good between us."

"That clock on the wall says it's almost eleven, and your growling stomach says you need to eat. Do you?"

"Mmm-hmm."

"So…" Zaf looked at her with concern and care and something that resembled love, but she quickly shook off the thought as post-orgasm fever. "Let's get you back into that sexy dress. I'm taking you out."

A poppin' party was throwing down at TreShawn's Spring Valley house. Cristal was on tap, guests stripped to their underwear and bling were playing Marco Polo in the pool, and the live music could probably be heard in the depths of the Mojave Desert.

But he'd disappeared. If any of the folks shooting his alcohol, eating his food or sopping up the luxury of the top-quality amenities his backbreaking career paid for were to notice he was missing, he'd be effing shocked.

A few teammates had hassled him to play host, and he had no one's ass to kick but his own for yielding. They'd survived the first day of training camp hell—cool. Opening his place in the city to teammates who didn't have the sense to R.I.C.E. their battered bodies in Desert Luck Center's residence hall wasn't his idea of a celebration.

Most of the people walking through his rooms and touching his shit were strangers—midprofile celebrities, riffraff blown in off the street, rented women with expert mouths and nightly rates.

Security would hold down Spanish Heights Drive— that was what he paid them for. Duncan Torsay on defense said he'd keep his own guests in line, but who knew if he would? TreShawn was no man's keeper. For all the brotherhood talk he'd heard during practices and meetings, he accepted that for every position there were at least two men each fighting to make it his. When the man breaking bread with you in the cafeteria was both your comrade and your adversary, there was no brotherhood.

Getting away wouldn't get him out of his head. Which was why he hadn't yet left his neighborhood. His Chevy

Suburban LTZ dominated the curb in front of a stucco two-story half the square footage of his house. Sitting on the hood, he sent a text message and craned his neck to search the darkened windows to see which would illuminate.

Arched balcony doors, he predicted, tossing his phone from hand to hand. There would be no reply text, just a slip of a woman poking her head out into the summer night to give him hell…before ultimately going along with whatever impulse he wanted her to get all wrapped up in.

A few minutes passed, and he paused, flipping over his phone to check to see if she'd replied, after all.

Nothing.

Weird. It was kissing midnight and she had a quirk about sleeping instead of compensating with early-morning energy drinks and B-12 shots. So she *had* to be home…right?

As he was about to slide off the truck's hood, the arched balcony doors glowed golden and the draperies swayed.

You're predictable, Min, he thought with an amused grin, leaning back against the windshield.

Minako Sato pushed open one of the doors and shot across the balcony. A curtain of jet-black hair swung back and forth over an orange hoodie. "Scenes like this should really be left to Shakespeare, Romeo," she said in that waspish tone she borrowed whenever his spontaneity shook up her routine.

"That'd make you Juliet? Nah." He chuckled. Minako would punch him if he accused her of being emotional, passionate or lovesick. "And I'm nobody's Romeo."

"I'll say," she served back, but their banter had diluted her irritation. "Romeo wouldn't blaze through Verona blasting—is that 'Moon River'?"

"Come out here and find out," he enticed.

"No. I have an early morning. As do you."

"Minako, I can just hang out here on the curb. But when I get bored with instrumentals, I might put the rap on."

"There's already plenty of rap coming from one of these party houses."

"That'd be mine."

"You're throwing a party? Wow. Just...wow." She sounded equal parts amazed and disappointed. "Good night, TreShawn. I'm getting back in bed, which is where I've been since the storm kicked out the power."

"The power's been back on for a while. It's early, even for you."

"Yeah, well, pharmacists perform best when well rested. I'd venture to say the same about athletes, but apparently, partying and playing works for you."

TreShawn's hands cushioned his head as he watched the sky. When the storm left, it'd taken the heavy clouds with it. Minuscule dots of silver filtered through as though someone had poked the sooty blanket with a needle. "Then I'll get comfortable here. Or you can come down and hear me out."

"Fine. I'm coming."

He was still in that position, watching the starry sky, when Minako rushed outside to the Suburban and confirmed, "You *are* listening to 'Moon River.' On repeat."

"You're surprised."

"We don't have the same taste in music. Now, if I can get you out of your superstar NFL player bubble long enough to watch *Breakfast at Tiffany's*, then you might actually be tolerable."

"I belong in that bubble." It was a dream and a nightmare, but he'd wanted it since he was a kid growing up poor in the ghetto.

"What are you doing here if you've got some VIP party going on at your place?"

Damn. The ice in her voice could give a man frostbite in the middle of summer. What was up with her?

He and Minako lived in the same neighborhood—they'd met months ago when her dog had slipped his leash and wound up peeing on TreShawn's garage door—but they moved on different wavelengths. She had a PhD, wore a white coat, was in bed by midnight. He was drafted to the NFL his senior year of college, had his name smeared through sports media and was the man to call on when you wanted to get messed up.

They were friends, though. She wasn't trying to claw into his world, and he liked having her within reach when the cameras and entourages got to be too much.

"I don't feel like entertaining folks," he told her.

Minako put her backside to the truck and looked up. "Then why order the food and hire the musicians and invite the guests?"

"Unwise decisions. Wasn't my idea, but nobody forced me to come into the city and unleash that—" he paused and the boom of bass beats surged through the air "—on the neighborhood."

"So shut it down. Ask everyone to leave." She turned toward him. When folks talked about having stars in their eyes, they usually didn't mean it literally. He thought it applied perfectly to the light reflected in Minako's deep-set eyes. They were usually behind a pair of plastic-framed glasses, and he guessed he'd never before tried to look closer than that. "I can't rescue you from your unwise party, TreShawn."

"I'm rescuing myself. That's why I split." When she lightly jabbed him in the ribs, he took her hand in his. The contrast reminded him of yin yang, and he liked that. "Come with me."

"Excuse me?"

"Come with me." He sat up, got a more complete look

at her. "The hoodie's all right, but you should probably change out of the Daffy Duck sweatpants."

"Donald."

"What?"

"Daffy's the naked *Looney Tunes* duck. Donald's the Disney duck with the sailor getup." She plucked at the fabric and seemed a little self-conscious. "Anyway, go home and find someone else to take off with you. I'm sure you'll find dozens of hot women tripping over themselves for you."

For his wallet, no doubt. "You're as hot as any of them. Plus, on second thought, the pants are kind of sexy."

Minako's starry-sky eyes widened—softened, even. "Serious?"

"Completely. Come with me. Let's hit up a club or a casino or something. 1 OAK in the Mirage. We might find you a man tonight."

"Oh." Minako wiggled her hand from his grip.

"So what's good with you?" TreShawn asked, hopping off the truck.

"Okay, I'll go. But I've got to check on Brewster and change my clothes first. Donald Duck pants aren't going to get me past the doorman at 1 OAK."

He laughed as she dashed back into her house. By the time she reemerged, he was in the driver's seat with the radio tuned to rap but at a volume that didn't have neighbors pressing their faces to the windows and eyeing him with consternation.

When he saw her, his hand slipped on the steering wheel and he thanked God the truck was still in Park.

Minako's glasses were in place and her hair hanging to her waist in a shiny sheet, but she looked *different*.

The slinky purple shirt was too tight—maybe that was it. Or the silver high heels too tall. Or the leather pants too…leather.

"Something wrong?" she asked, coming up to his window, then glancing back at her house. "Concern is written all over this." She circled her hand in front of her face.

The lipstick, he thought, his attention bolting to her devil-red mouth. That had to be the anomaly. Minako didn't paint her lips. She was all about balm and she smelled like peaches whenever she rubbed the stuff on.

She didn't smell like peaches as she climbed into the passenger's seat and put her purse down at her feet.

"You smell like chocolate," he said.

"Oh—yeah." She snorted. "I ate a candy bar on the way out."

"Aren't you eating when we get to the club?"

"Of course." She peeled back her lips. "Do I have Hershey's in my teeth?"

He clicked on the interior lights and inspected. "All clear. You look…"

"What?"

"I don't know." He couldn't piece together a thought that'd make sense. In that outfit she'd have no problem cruising past doormen at any of Vegas's clubs. But she wasn't the beanie-hats-and-flat-shoes Minako he was used to. He'd come to her because he could always count on her to look the same, act the same, be the same.

"Whenever you're ready…" She pointed to the steering wheel.

Ready for stuff to spin, change and drift out of control again? No, he wasn't. Life had started to level out after the Chargers traded him to the Slayers last season, but he had spent too much time in steroids-withdrawal fog and still hadn't broken away from his usual crowd. He was close enough to hang with the friends he'd cut up with when he was in California. And as his uncle had told him, he was only as good as the company he kept.

As far as off-field friendships, he had very few—and

wasn't all that assured in the genuineness of most of them. A couple of veterans on the team were solid and up for anything. The team's female trainer, Charlotte, she was all right, but she had a man who was getting most of her time now. That left TreShawn with the hipster neighborhood girl whose Doberman had a nasty habit of marking territory that didn't belong to him.

But if he lost Minako...

"One of these days," she said as he pulled off the curb, "I'm not going to be there to save you from yourself."

She was here tonight, though, fiddling around with his radio because it irked him and talking over the music, anyway, and that had to be his solace.

1 OAK was at Friday night capacity. Minako chose the room. Immediately, they let the killin' DJ coax them into dancing, then he treated her to a burger and they settled at the bar with a bottle of vodka. The high energy and jazzed crowd let him pretend he could be anonymous for a couple of hours.

"Is this really as excellent as I think it is, or is the whopping price tag influencing my taste buds?" Minako asked, setting her lipstick-stained glass on the bar and twisting around the Cîroc to read the label.

"It's excellent vodka," he confirmed.

"I'm still baffled that you spent hundreds of bucks just to drink with me. A Big Gulp would've been okay." She took another swallow. "Oooh, that's perfect."

TreShawn chuckled. She was real in everything she did. No facades or hidden agendas. He was about to fill his glass when he saw a toss of golden-brown hair and beauty that dudes he'd studied in college wrote poems about.

"*Tsk, tsk, tsk.* Look at your thirsty ass," he heard Minako say, and he found her wearing an I-know-what-you're-doing smirk and shaking her head.

"What're you talking about?"

"Just saying, I'd put this bottle in front of you, but you're not thirsty for a drink. You know her?"

"Met her," he acknowledged, glancing at Joey de la Peña again. Wrapped in tight silk, she leaned against the bar. At Desert Luck she'd carried around a cane, but he couldn't see it with stools and people obstructing his view. "She's a narc. She's involved in some drug program the front office put together for camp."

"Ah. Did someone fail the test?"

"The annual pissing event hasn't happened yet," he told her, holding Joey in his sights.

"Pretty. You aim high, don't you?" Minako cocked her head. "I think she's alone. Let's go say hi."

"You're not going," he said, turning her back to the bar when she swiveled on her stool.

"Why not? She knows drugs, I know drugs—we can talk shop. Or are you afraid I'll tell her you want to have plenty of sex and babies with her?" She shrugged at his withering glare. "Fine, abandon the woman you brought here and go to her."

TreShawn hesitated. "Are you mad?"

"No." She smiled, lifted her drink. "Really, go to her. We're at 1 OAK. I won't be lonely."

He took the vodka bottle—which earned him a double take from Minako—and made his way to Joey.

"Care for some Cîroc?" he offered, his voice competing with the ear-ringing noise. Joey leaned close and he repeated the question.

"I don't have a glass."

"Consider that problem solved," he said, snagging the bartender's attention.

"I shouldn't, TreShawn," she said, and he got the impression she was talking about something other than a drink. "Um, I wouldn't have expected to see any Slayers out and about after what I observed at camp today. Aren't you hurting?"

"We push the pain down." Using a different approach, he asked, "Why aren't men lined up to give you anything you want?"

"This deters them, usually. They ask me to dance, and I can't." She reached behind her and presented the cane. "Uh, actually, I'm with—"

"Their loss," he decided. "If you want to go to a couch, I can chill with you. Another option is this. A party's going down at my place."

"You're throwing a party but you're here?"

"Yes. I'm willing to go back if you'll be my guest."

Joey smiled. He couldn't read it—had *no* clue what she was thinking—but he didn't care because it was the sexiest thing this night had to offer. "What might I find at your party that I can't get here, TreShawn?"

Privacy, he almost said. In his mind he could see himself trailing a hand through her hair and laying a kiss on her that'd clear away the hesitation pushing them apart.

Would it take her by surprise? Would she roll with it?

Again, he saw himself touching her, but this was reality. His platinum chronograph watch shone under the bar lights, and the sparkle seemed to spin as he watched his fingers brush the pattern of a loose curl hanging over her cheek.

Last night they'd established that he didn't invite her onto the practice field because he wanted to hit on her. But that was then, this was now. Now he was hitting on her, seducing her, whatever anyone wanted to call it. Because he couldn't pull himself back.

"We can ignore your cane. Put it behind you again and forget all about it. We don't need to dance."

"TreShawn...wait..." Joey shook her head. "I can't. I'm sorry."

"The Slayers, the Blues, nobody needs to know if you want it like that."

"You don't understand—" Her eyes fixed on something behind him and she waved. A tall guy—Middle Eastern, he'd guess—came out of the background.

"TreShawn, this is my boyfriend, Zaf. Zaf, TreShawn's the Slayers' kicker. He told me he's looking to break records this season. I think he'll make this city's sports fanatics proud."

"Hey, good to meet you," the man said easily. "I know some folks who're deep in Fantasy Football. Your name comes up."

Zaf curled an arm around Joey's shoulders, and, like her, allowed an unreadable smile. But the meaning behind his gesture hollered, *This is mine. Don't get too close to what's mine.*

So Minako's dog wasn't the only one unafraid to mark his territory.

"Break records, huh?" Zaf said conversationally.

TreShawn didn't trust his casual tone. There was a cagey quality about him *and* Joey, if he wanted to reflect on it more. Except he now knew her secret—she had a man, and TreShawn was wasting his time with her.

Or was he? She hadn't rejected him until she saw her man in the club. Maybe she wasn't happy and wanted a way out.

"Hall of Fame," TreShawn said to Zaf. "I put down my stamp now and focus on excellence straight to the end, then I'll be in the ranks of Stenerud."

"Stenerud. A pure kicker."

"You know football?"

"I pick up things here and there." Zaf stroked Joey's arm. "Table's ready."

"Okay." Joey gazed up at the guy, twisting her hand in his shirt, and damn TreShawn if he didn't sense a sexual intensity between them. They'd either just screwed or would very, very soon.

When they left the bar, he pushed the vodka bottle back to the bartender for disposal. He didn't want it, didn't want to be here, didn't want to go home, either.

Minako said she wouldn't be lonely, but she was sitting alone when he returned to her end of the bar. "I suppose not every woman is destined to fall for your charms?" she surmised, sucking on a slice of fruit.

"She has a man."

"And you backed off? Well, that's a compliment to your character, TreShawn."

He almost told her to hold off on declaring him a jolly good fellow, but she was beaming at him and leading him to the dance floor, and it felt kind of nice to have someone think he was a better man than he could possibly be.

Chapter 8

"Gian DiGorgio's making a move."

Zaf was standing at the range scrambling eggs with a whisk when the text had come through. Waiting for Joey's response, he sent his contact a quick response.

"What kind of move?" she called out to him from the recesses of the house. Hardly a week ago she'd put a house key in his hand, and they were settled into a routine. Playing house, they had sex but bunked in separate rooms, shared mundane conversations snuggled up on the leather sofa, took turns fixing meals. He went with her to a physical therapy appointment—the highlight of that being taught how to oil-massage her hip at home. She found excuses to hang back at the house while he was pulling out the guest room's original shelving system, and on those days he didn't get any work done without tussling around naked with her first. It was similar to how they'd been in DC, except they'd always slept together then. More was at stake now, more guards up—and they weren't in love.

Joey wasn't, at least. Love for her poisoned Zaf, and he let it because the torture of wanting to have a right to her but knowing he couldn't was karma he deserved.

Today they would be apart—she had appointments at ODC and Slayers Stadium, he had a meeting with a former DiGorgio Royal Casino employee—and wouldn't see each other until early evening at some bridal boutique where she'd be fitted for a gown.

A dress shop, or any place that had something to do with women's apparel, threatened to trigger hives, but she had agreed to join the bride's crew and their dates for dinner and he wouldn't leave her unaccompanied. As her "boyfriend," he should be there. As her protector, he'd be damned if anyone kept him away.

He was already pissed enough that Joey wouldn't let him come with her to the stadium or the training camp facility where she was putting in time. A few days ago DiGorgio had entered Desert Luck Center unauthorized and touched Joey's shoulder, claiming he had a wedding gift for his godson's fiancée.

Charlotte Blue had refused to speak to him. His other godson, Santino Franco, a new hire on the team's coaching staff, had ordered security to escort DiGorgio off the premises.

Zaf thought the wedding gift was a pretense, a message that taunted if he couldn't get to Joey at home, he would find another way.

"A lawsuit," Zaf told her, when he could tamp rage down deep enough to allow him to find his voice again. "Civil bullshit against the city. Defamation of character, other stuff. He's claiming that as a result of being falsely arrested, he suffered financial loss and irreparable damage to his reputation as a businessman."

He turned off the burner, took the skillet away.

Joey appeared in the doorway, giving him an incredulous stare. "The bastard runs criminal activity out of his casino, orders a hit on his friend, stalks me and he wants to get paid *on top of* escaping charges?"

"His investors are pulling out of the casino. Celebrities are gun-shy. It's more of a variety show punch line than an exclusive Vegas attraction. Hurting his prized casino's like kicking him in the balls. He probably already has the means and money to rebuild his empire, but why do it on his own dime when he can get the city to foot the bill for him? He's riding high on a power trip, but I think most of the erratic behavior is desperation. He's sloppy."

"I don't like that. Erratic behavior and desperation can get people killed." Absentmindedly she turned her weapon in her hand.

"If you bring a gun to breakfast, what the hell do you take to bed with you?" Zaf was partly messing with her—but he remained standing with a frying pan full of fluffy steaming scrambled eggs, waiting for her answer.

Joey set the handgun on the counter next to the economy-size jar of Jelly Belly he'd finally got around to buying as a replacement for the candy he'd swiped his first night here. Her stark white shirt was a little too transparent for his liking, since she was planning to go to ODC and a football stadium. He wanted her to stick around and let him undo those smooth plain buttons with his teeth.

"I take my iPad to bed with me," she admitted, reaching up to whip her hair into the sexiest messy ponytail he'd ever seen. "But my locked and loaded fella here is always close by. Closer now, circumstances as they are."

"I'm not going to let anyone—*anyone*—hurt you, Jo."

"You can't be with me every minute, Zaf. My fella can." Her smile failed to conquer the fear and tension. He didn't regret coming out of hiding for her. He didn't regret rejoining society just to protect her. But if he wasn't careful, what price would she pay this time? "And it's not every day a hot guy invades my house and fixes me breakfast."

Joey puckered her mouth, winced. "You didn't hear me say that."

It was Zaf's turn to smile, and his was legit. He grabbed a fork from the counter and handed it to her. "Eat. And yeah, I heard you call me sexy."

"I did not." She snatched the fork and scooped up some eggs from the skillet. "I said hot."

"I know."

She laughed. "Zaf…"

He held the skillet, waiting again. Would she let him stay here, ready to hold her up if she wanted him to? Or would she keep leaning on that cane and push him away because he was the reason for it?

Did he have any right to pray that she'd look past what he'd done?

"Zaf," she repeated, shaking her head as she took another bite of eggs. *"Gracias."*

"Did you just thank me?"

Joey put the fork in the skillet and, swallowing, looked him dead in the eye. Her tongue traced her bottom lip, and then, "I could say it again. Or I could show you."

He set the skillet aside, coming back to her with a kiss on her forehead. "Show me."

"Oh… You're hard already."

"What time is ODC expecting you?" He was already unbuttoning her shirt, undoing her efforts to boldly take on the outside world when, according to her moaning whispers last night, she'd rather stay underneath him.

"Nine." Joey unzipped his jeans, picked his pockets for a condom. "But they know I'm bringing pastries."

Zaf carried her to the sofa. With her propped carefully on his lap, he sank into smooth leather before his cock sank into her. "So you can be a few minutes late and they'll stop caring once you hand over the goods?"

"It means they'll—*ohhh*!" She began to move on his lap, pressing her hands into the sofa, biting down on her bottom lip until it came away red and plump and ready for his kiss.

"It means what?" he prodded when he released her mouth. One hand guided her ass while the other plucked her bra out of his way. Sucking in a nipple, leaving it dark and wet, he said, "Tell me, Jo."

"I swear you're evil. You can't expect me to hold a real conversation when you're doing—*ah, mmm, damn it*!" She tried to put her hand between them to control the intensity but he moved it aside and let her sexy scream reverberate inside him. "When you're doing this."

"You mean doing you?"

She started to laugh but it was lost in a gasp when he moved her in such a way that her clit rubbed up and down his shaft. Her orgasm gripped him and as she constricted around his flesh while moaning in his ear, he came violently in the condom.

Sighing together, holding each other, they waited for the aftershocks to ease. Zaf trashed the condom then helped her to her feet and righted her bra. "Get out of here, slacker."

"Ha," she said. "You're a bad influence. I have a full day in front of me."

"I've got a full day, too. It's going to be a sweaty one. The shelves and the plaster for your closet came in early. Your shoes are going to get their dream home sooner than we figured."

"The hot guy who invaded my house and fixed breakfast is going to be wearing a tool belt? I'll pass on the stressful day and stay here."

"Uh-uh. You should be good and mellow to take it on,

coming as hard as you did. Think that orgasm will last you until we see each other again later, or do I need to touch you up right quick?"

"I'll last," she said, but her gaze dropped to his crotch, as though she was on second thought considering a *touch up.* "Okay, now I need to wash up and get out the door."

In the kitchen, he sat on the counter and picked up his coffee mug.

"Zaf, how did you know about Gian DiGorgio's lawsuits? They're not public knowledge. I've been having someone in the Bureau keep an eye on developments before the media can detect it. You're ahead of even that person."

The coffee had grown colder than he liked it, but he swallowed the caffeine to buy a moment to think. Living with Joey was great in that it allowed him the proximity to do his job, yet outmaneuvering her daily was taxing. She followed him when he stepped away to take private phone calls, asked questions that were difficult to circumvent without outright deceiving her—and somehow he'd gotten to a place where he hated resorting to deceit when it came to her.

"Different intelligence sources rake in different information. That's nothing unusual, Jo."

She shut off the faucet, bunched a drying towel in her hands and observed him with reproach. "Are you lying to me? And to say you're not when in fact you are—that's a lie, too."

"Am I lying about the inconsistency between intelligence sources? No, Josephine, I'm not."

Tossing the towel, she and her cane closed in. "Are you leading me away from my question to avoid answering me straight-on?"

"I keep a trusted network, and not everyone in that network is a part of the Bureau. I'm not a part of the Bureau anymore, so does it even make a difference?"

"Sometimes," she said, "I feel you're holding back information I should know. The secrecy, the suspicious phone calls, the times you disappear from this house with your computer when you think I'm not paying attention. So tell me. If you're not Archangel back in the line of duty, are you hacking again?"

Hacking had first gotten him expelled from high school for altering attendance records and grade reports at the well-paid request of classmates. The expulsion had resulted in his being hired by a top-tier corporate attorney under the table, and that had led to him to losing the riches he'd accumulated when he was arrested, tried and convicted for his offenses.

A prison term had encouraged him to rethink his career as a computer criminal for hire. The military had reformed him and he'd fought for the other side of the law. As of late his security expertise paid the bills and then some, but the jobs he booked were few. For five years he'd kept himself hidden and untraceable, and only one of the most privileged in his field had been able to convince him to rejoin civilization for something other than a lead concerning his cousin's killers.

Avenging the death of a kid left in his care had been Zaf's driving force for so long that it felt unnatural to put any other priority first. Every day he quietly questioned whether or not his presence in Joey's life was a hindrance. He cared about her, wanted to do right by her, but hadn't those intentions always led to needless bloodshed?

"I'm not tapping anyone's systems to put cash in my pocket," he told her.

"What are you doing that can take you away from me again?" Joey cursed, backed up. "Forget I said that. I shouldn't have said that."

"I'm not here, Jo. Not really. So I can't be taken away." A freakin' liar was what he'd become. He was here, with Joey, in every way. But the second she resurrected her love for him was the second he added to the danger he was here to defuse.

"I said forget it."

"Joey, I have people in place in DiGorgio's circle. Household staff, casino personnel, security experts. I can't compromise the identities of these people while they still have lives to defend."

"What does *that* mean?"

"Someone fell." The words sort of dangled in the air, and he put down his coffee mug. "It was Wilcox Smitz."

He watched through hooded eyes as she connected the name to the dead man. "Wilcox was the man DiGorgio hired to kill Alessandro Franco in Italy. He was on my payroll and I had him in place to intercept the job. DiGorgio managed to put some fear into him and Wilcox recanted every word of his confession—"

"Before taking a cyanide capsule." Smitz nullified his statement and committed suicide instead of putting faith in WITSEC relocation. This combined with the court's decision to toss the video footage Zaf had collected that contained Alessandro Franco's confession detailing DiGorgio's misdeeds, had enabled DiGorgio to walk as a free man.

Explaining this to Joey, patiently managing the conversation when she frequently interrupted, he felt her start to distance herself. The magnitude of it all began to settle.

"You were in Italy a few months ago," she said slowly. "Franco was a fugitive then. So you found him, taped his confession, then instead of alerting the authorities or his family to his whereabouts, you allowed him to almost die. And somehow your name never came up."

"I made sure one of my people picked up the order. He wasn't going to be murdered."

"Zaf, he tried to kill himself because he thought someone else was going to do it." She scrunched her face. "How can you tell me all of this so calmly? So mechanically? You say you're not capable of love, but do you have a heart at all?"

"I had what I needed to put DiGorgio away."

"Except it didn't do any good in the end. That's why you're here, isn't it? To perform cleanup?" She buttoned her shirt and fussed with her ponytail, which had been messy to begin with. "He's following me around because he knows he's untouchable. Your plan was a deadly one. It failed and it's too late for damage control."

Zaf stoically absorbed every word. What she said wasn't anything he hadn't already told himself. It was her right to be angry. He could handle it, but he had no intention of setting aside his mission now that she knew he'd been more than a man watching DiGorgio from a distance.

"I can only pray to Mary that your *protection* doesn't send me to the morgue," she said bitterly, taking her cake carrier from the counter and limping to the entryway.

"Let me help you put that in your car," he said.

"No. I can handle this." Without looking back, she added, "Don't come to the boutique today. I'll be safe with my friends."

"Be mad if you want, but I can't agree to that."

"I don't *want* to be mad. I don't want to feel as if I'm having sex with a stranger. I don't want to wonder if every other sentence you say is a lie or part of some grand plan you have going. I swear to you, I don't want to think about the destruction and casualties your way of thinking can leave in the wake. So agree, Zaf. I'll be trying on a dress then having dinner with my friends. I won't need your services tonight."

"What do you need, then?"

"Space. Time. I need to know if I can forgive you for this. A man ultimately killed himself and another tried to because of your crazy risky plan. You've been with me for days now, inside my house, inside me, and you didn't tell me until I pried the truth out of you. That hurts me, Zaf."

"Knowing or not knowing doesn't change the reality that DiGorgio has been watching you."

"It's not your business to filter my knowledge. You don't get to pick and choose what information I take in. I'm not a child and I'm not simple."

"You're not entitled to every detail of the things I've done and the reasons why," he served back.

"Oh? So you'll have your secrets and I'll have mine?"

"That's how it is. Just because I'm not prying the truth out of you doesn't mean I don't know what kind of job the Blues hired you for."

Her shoulders slumped, but only for a fraction of a moment before she shot back, "It's no secret that I'm part of the team's anti-drug abuse program."

"Don't try to snow a man who can see right through you. I familiarized myself with the Blues. They care about the shield and their business interests. Their style isn't to hold their men's hands. If anyone's violating a drug policy, Marshall Blue and his wife probably want to cut 'em. Camp numbers are inflated. As good as any player is, there's someone else ready and able to take his place. So what I think they hired you to do is weed out the users."

"A pun, now? Not very funny."

"Wasn't meant to be. Take it however the hell you want, but they aren't paying you to tout the virtues of a drug-free lifestyle. They want you to find out who's abusing so they can clean things up. Am I right or am I right?"

"Be quiet."

Nerve struck, but he wasn't done.

"That's why you're suddenly a fixture at NFL social events and hanging back at camp long after the Good Samaritan group wraps up, isn't it?" Zaf knew a double agent when he came across one, and she was carrying out her orders to the letter—buddying up to the players and staff, going off to check-in meetings with the team's owners. "That's why you let TreShawn Dibbs box you in at the bar that night in the Mirage, isn't it?"

He'd noticed *that*, too. At first perception, he hadn't liked the picture of the guy touching her. But her body language and the almost clinical way she reacted to Dibbs's flirting was reminiscent of the technique she used when she was undercover.

Whether she was working a cover or not, Zaf didn't appreciate another man touching his woman. It wasn't fair of him to feel possessive, particularly when he couldn't provide the life she deserved. He'd never been good about sharing.

"What if the thing with TreShawn is genuine?" she challenged quietly. "If I like having the attention of a man who doesn't remind me of my cane and my limp?"

"A man who makes it easy for you to lie to yourself?"

"Zaf, of all the men who approach me, I would estimate about ninety percent of them lose interest when they realize I carry a stick. It's a symbol of damage and neediness, I suppose, and it sucks major *huevos*."

So he reminded her of her vulnerabilities, and TreShawn Dibbs helped her forget them. "Be honest with me, Jo. Do you want to forget reality all the time, or are you letting him circle you because you think he's a name you can turn in to the Blues?"

"I…I don't know, Zaf."

"Yeah? I think you do, deep down where'd you need to dig, and dig hard, to find it. You left that club with me.

You remember what we did before we ended up there, and what we did when we came back here."

He did, in tormenting vivid detail. Being with her wore him out, wrung him out, and he couldn't see himself ever getting enough of it.

"When it comes to that," she said, "you're the only one. You're the only one getting that part of me."

"Would that still be true if giving that part of you to Dibbs or anyone else could score you a name to turn in to the Blues?"

"*¡Cállate!* I won't listen to you tear me down when I am doing nothing wrong."

"Nothing illegal. An agenda can be legal but still all kinds of wrong."

"Really? Just consider, then, that if you believed that five years ago, I wouldn't have been shot." She sighed. "I don't want to do this. I don't want to keep throwing this in your face. It hurts you and it hurts me."

"I'm a hypocritical bastard. I get it. But I don't want to see you make the mistakes I did."

"Why do you care so much if you never loved me?"

Zaf wouldn't answer that. She'd already extracted so much from him, and he wouldn't compromise her further by rattling her judgment. Giving her reasons to love him would accomplish just that. She was sharper—they both were—when emotions were in check.

"Listen to me. DiGorgio was watching you before I got involved," he said gravely. "That's *why* I got involved." He had been called from his self-perpetuated exile for her. From the beginning, it had been about guarding her.

"Are you giving me reasons why now?" She turned to face him. "Why go to such lengths for a woman you never loved?"

Zaf hopped off the counter and paused in front of her as he left the kitchen. "Before you ask that question again, give yourself some space and time to think about what the answer might be and decide if you're ready to handle that kind of truth."

"Zaf—"

"Get going, Jo. It's half past nine."

Some secrets were a woman's to keep.

Joey didn't believe in letting any man dictate her schedule—even the fake boyfriend in charge of ensuring her safety—and figured Zaf would persuade her to cancel her spur-of-the-moment lunch plans if he knew about them, so she'd kept mum when he asked her what she had lined up for the day.

Their fight still ringing through her system, she was glad she had followed her instinct to do whatever the hell she wanted because this was still *her* life.

In front of CCL, she saw the man from before. Same corduroy pants, which appeared soiled with mud now. Around him, people spilled out of the library as others pursued it. Those who didn't pretend to not see him passed with glances that ranged from suspicious to irritated to repulsed.

She didn't feel sorry for him. She felt ashamed of the others—and herself, for having put cash in his hand with the belief that it would impact his life in some meaningful way. Climbing the steps with her tote bag hanging off a shoulder and her cane reflecting the merciless sunlight, she greeted him, "Any room for me on that step?"

"Well, hello, friend." The man scooted over and she settled next to him, much to the bewilderment and annoyance of the patrons coming and going. "Back again? You were here yesterday."

Joey shook her head, holding concern at bay. The man likely wouldn't take too kindly to a "poor you" look. "No, it's been longer than that. The days go by faster now, it seems. When I was a kid, summers were endless. Barn chores in the morning, horseback riding in the afternoon and superslow nights of sneaking lemonade from the fridge and watching fireflies out the window." She smiled at the simplicity of those Texas summers. "I whined and complained about being bored, but my friend and I always found a way to get ourselves into trouble. We made our own excitement. All that's changed now." She spied him, then retrieved a Nickel's sub sandwich from her bag and unwrapped it on her lap. Taking half for herself, she gave him the other. "What were summers like for you when you were a kid?"

"Same as yours," he said. "Horses and chores and the like. I grew up on a farm. You?"

"A ranch."

"My buddies and I rode like the wind on bikes. We used to play baseball—modified, though. Instead of baseballs, we used melons. Instead of bats, we used lumber. Got a lot of splinters that way."

She smiled at that and they ate in silence for several minutes.

"Aren't you going in the library?" he asked.

"Nope, not today."

Realization blossomed in his eyes. "You made the trip just to share a sandwich with me?"

"I was hungry and was hoping you might join me." She crushed the wrapper and brushed crumbs off her pants. "How are you coming along with the Copernicus biography?"

"I finished it."

"Yeah?"

"Four times already. A librarian gave it to me and asked me to keep it."

"Kind librarian." Providing it was an act of kindness

and not a gesture to shoo him out of the building. "So where do you usually read your books?"

"Here."

"Las Vegas is a far cry from farm life," Joey said gently. "Where are you, usually, when the fireflies come out?"

"Waiting for them."

Meaning he slept outside? Then he was homeless. "When it rains and there's lightning, where are you?" she pushed, needing to know, needing to find a way to lead him to better circumstances.

"I think these are getting to be rude questions," he said, and his lucidity was a startling contrast to his fuzzy demeanor when she'd sat down. Then again, he'd just put some solid food in his belly, so perhaps the sustenance was starting to help clear his mind.

"That's not my intention," she said, but she wasn't sorry for prying if it'd help him get off the street and into a shelter with a bed and a shower and access to three squares a day. "I should go. But I think I'll be back tomorrow around this time to eat my lunch."

He considered her with those rheumy eyes under deeply hooded lids, and nodded. "You might be in the mood for soup and a baguette. There's a place down the way here on Flamingo that makes a nice-tasting lemon chicken soup."

"Thanks for the rec." Her memory fell back to the afternoon she'd met him and how she'd mentally cringed at the potato chip he had given her with his bare hand. Now, humbled, she outstretched her hand and decided she wouldn't be offended if he didn't accept it. "I'm Joey."

"Cliff."

When he shook her hand and she made her way down the steps, she was a little reluctant to leave. Sitting in front of a library, sharing a sandwich with a stranger, was an escape. For a short while she hadn't thought about researching controlled pharmaceuticals, sniffing out substance-abusing athletes or outmaneuvering a disgruntled casino owner with the riches of a pharaoh.

She *had* thought about Zaf. Lately she held him in her mind. It must have everything to do with close proximity and the peculiar way his tense energy melded with hers. Their hearts communicated, she was certain of that.

Yet, in anger she'd asked him if he had a heart.

She friggin' hated the way they'd left things this morning. They were both guilty of putting too much out there and unleashing emotion that would do neither of them any good.

More than that, she hated not being in on his secrets. The Arizona bust crumbled because he hadn't trusted her with the important-as-all-hell detail that he was wearing a mask and there was another layer to their mission. They'd been in love but where was the trust?

Oh, but wait. The love had been one-sided then.

As she turned the Ferrari's engine and headed for the posh bridal boutique where her friends waited, she tried to block a new suspicion. Fear, really. It had already formed, though, and now she knew—the love was *still* one-sided.

Chapter 9

Bubbly went a long way toward revitalizing Joey's pep and good cheer. After one delicate flute's worth had teased her system, she remained mostly unaffected and stuck on the angry argument she'd left unresolved. So she had another, graciously nodding from a fainting couch in LJD's Couture Brides' drawing room when one of Leda J. Dawson's assistants addressed her. "More champagne, Miss de la Peña?"

Joey was weighing the pros and cons of a third glass when Temperance Blue used her mother-of-the-bride authority to cut her off and switch her to a choice of mineral water or Panama-imported coffee.

"The beverage selection is superior, that's true, but try not to consume too much now," Tem advised in her cloud-soft voice as she beckoned the assistant to take away the Boërl and Kroff on its polished platter. "Our timeline doesn't give us much leeway for adjustments and alterations, so today's measurements will need to be spot-on.

Do you have a tendency to bloat? Because I'll have to ask you to refrain from sampling the juice, as well."

"But…" Joey indicated Charlotte's bridesmaids, sprinkled throughout the drawing room that looked more appropriate to host elegant balls than house wedding gowns. A couple of the women had just returned from their fittings in the back of the salon, and the rest waited to be pulled and stuffed and pinched and cinched. "They're drinking juice. Martha has milk."

"Martha's child is apparently as dramatic as she is, and has given the girl heartburn. Only dairy offers any relief—though I think it's a convenient excuse to overindulge in ice cream and cheesecake and whatever else she's unwisely introducing to her baby. Honestly, she's rolling the dice, and it's by the grace of God that her body has the genetics to resist that kind of overeating."

The woman in question stood between her sisters, the tallest of the three Blue girls, a vision of perfect pregnancy health. Her melon-sized baby bump was covered with a short fluttery dress, and apparently her feet weren't too swollen to deprive her of fashionable high heels.

Martha broke away from the huddle to go to her teenage foster daughter, who was ogling a rather risqué designer gown displayed in a lighted curio cabinet.

Charlotte was Joey's best friend, but how she admired Martha Ryder's boldness and courage to go for what she wanted—despite a fierce and sort of oppressive mother standing in her way at every critical turn.

"I'd say she and her doctors are in the best position to determine what is and isn't healthy for her baby," Joey told Tem firmly, though she accepted a glass of mineral water with a peaceful smile.

No use pissing the woman off twice in a single day. Earlier at the Slayers' administrative offices, she had informed Tem and Marshall that she'd had knowledge of

TreShawn Dibbs's party—so did the media, though no arrests or other complications had come of it, and they'd swiftly lost interest. When she admitted she'd turned down the player's invitation, thereby throwing away the opportunity to scan the place for illegal substances, the Blues had all but lost their shit.

TreShawn's infamous reputation clung to him, and there was added concern about the possibility of his contaminating the roster. Charlotte's friendship with him could, and likely would, push her into a precarious position.

So Joey agreed to take him up on his next invitation. In all likelihood there wouldn't be another. At the club in the Mirage, his flirting and her rejection had been unmistakable. She'd introduced Zaf as her boyfriend, and if TreShawn was a stand-up guy, he wouldn't tempt her to visit his place, and he definitely wouldn't try to kiss her again.

Another few seconds and it might've happened if she hadn't turned her face or if Zaf's arrival hadn't brought things back into clarity.

In fact, it had been during that moment, when she stood at the bar with a good-looking athlete in front of her and the man from the darkest chapter of her past in the background, that she'd tested the waters of escaping her reality. TreShawn made her feel desired, sexy and as whole as any other woman—but their connection was false. When Zaf had stepped into her sights, she'd *known*.

Zaf didn't let her ignore her cane and who she was now. He was the brightest and most devastating part of her, and damn Miz Willa for correctly pegging her as someone who was in love but didn't want to be.

This was Joey's life, and she had the final say-so in whether or not she would allow him to leave footprints on her heart again.

"I can't do that."

"Pardon me?" Tem sipped from her own champagne flute.

"Nothing. My mind wandered."

"Then I was right to switch you to water."

"Has everyone arrived?" This from the bride whisperer herself, Leda J. Dawson. She was Wedding Gown Expert Barbie brought to life, with meticulously trimmed blond hair and clear blue eyes that seemed to encourage "Just lend me your troubles, darlin'."

Leda greeted everyone individually, chatting briefly with the ladies she'd previously met. The only newcomers were Joey and Martha's foster daughter, Avery.

"We have a stylist specifically for Avery," the woman said, adding an enchanting smile. "The others are here for final measurements. A last-minute maid of honor isn't typical, but some of my most brilliant work has come from unconventional situations. Besides, our bride is quite an independent one, and she doesn't wish to overburden you with duties. Essentially, we need to get you fitted, accessorized and review your ceremony duties concerning the train, bouquet, et cetera."

"Great. Let's all go check out the dress—"

"Might I have a moment with you first? I'd like to give you a tour and explain the palette. Catch you up."

"Weddings have palettes?" Joey asked as Leda summoned her from the fainting couch, and the woman looked flabbergasted.

"Leda's approach is very artistic," Tem contributed, sending them off with a wave of her flawlessly manicured hand. "I imagine you'll want a wedding of your own after touring this salon."

That was laughable, being she had no genuine romantic prospects willing to slip a ring on her finger even if she'd allow it. Though she did pause, captivated, at a glimmering glass case displaying gowns, veils and jewelry Leda

J. Dawson's grandmother had designed during the Truman administration.

The place held suites reserved for brides' entourages. Charlotte's suite resembled a fancy old-fashioned sitting room. A pedestal and stepstool sat in the center. A pin board covered half of a wall, and it was cluttered with designs, handwritten notes, fabric swatches and photographs of venues, flowers and hairstyles.

"It's a lot, isn't it?" Charlotte said, entering the room and joining Joey and Leda in front of the pin board.

"It's kind of perfect." If the actual event even partly resembled the board, it would be an unforgettably beautiful affair. "So this is really, seriously happening. Charlotte Blue and Nate Franco are getting married."

"Yup, that's what the invitations say." Charlotte smiled, but there was a question in it. *Are things going okay?*

Since Gian DiGorgio's unwanted presence at Desert Luck Center, Charlotte had begun to check in with her more often, and she'd come close to telling her fiancé everything.

Joey nodded as if to say, "I'm all right."

"I'm glad you're here, Joey. Nate is, too. We wanted you to be a part of this."

"Hey, no sappy talk right now. My eye makeup is on point."

"It certainly is," Leda agreed with approval. "And not to worry about smudging anything. You made a wise choice to wear a button-down top, and you'll be stepping into your gown."

She was referencing the miniature debacle that had happened a short while ago when the first bridesmaid, Charlotte's college friend Krissy O'Claire-Lewis, had tried to tug her clinging crewneck shirt over an eight-months-preggers belly, glasses and an uncontrollable mane of curly hair. What made matters worse was her baby started dancing on her bladder while she was struggling to free herself.

Fortunately, someone had been able to rescue her from disaster and mortification that would've likely caused permanent social damage.

"Shall I get the design now?" Leda asked Charlotte.

"Please." When Leda strode away, Charlotte told Joey, "You're already aware that your maid of honor gown will vary slightly from the bridesmaids dresses, but I asked Leda to design something in addition."

Joey touched her hair. "Don't say it's a tiara. It takes a unique kind of grace to pull off a tiara, and I'm just not the type."

"Oh… Well, first, we did have a tiara in mind for you, so we'll go ahead and nix that. Second, you totally do have grace, but we'll analyze that another time. Third, that's not what I was referring to." Charlotte motioned to Leda, who revealed an image on her tablet.

A cane. But it had the flair and kick-ass quality of a royal scepter, and was by far more glamorous than any accessory she owned. It was ornamental, breathtaking. According to the notes, it was to be made of white gold and embellished with amethyst gemstones and diamonds.

"Lottie—it's too—I can't possibly—" She made grabby hands for the tablet. "I love it. And you. You're the *best* best friend a girl could ask for."

"Yay!" Charlotte clapped her hands. "So in addition to being fitted for your gown, you'll be measured for the cane. We want to make sure it's ergonomic. Oh, and like your everyday canes, this one will be adjustable."

"You considered everything."

"Hey, I'm just a bride looking out for her crew. Since you're hosting a wicked bridal shower that'll scandalize my mom, I figured I owed you this."

Leda tsked. "Shame on you," she said, but with a smirk.

"Don't warn her," Charlotte said.

"I won't. I told Tem when she commissioned me for this wedding that my allegiance is to the bride." She fluffed her hair. "But it'd be nice to find myself with an invitation to this scandalizing event. There *will* be buff strippers, won't there?"

"Absolutely," Joey assured, while Charlotte stared.

"Miss Blue, don't look at me like that. I'm a professional artist. I appreciate the male physique. It's a beautiful thing, especially when it's wearing nothing but a G-string."

"I think you were a nice, sweet bridal consultant before you met the lot of us," Charlotte said to Leda. "We corrupted you, didn't we? Was it Martha? She's the freakiest of us all… Wait, no, Joey is."

Joey cheered as the others laughed. "Thank you, thank you. It's an honor."

"We'll take the cane measurement now," Leda decided, touching a finger to the corner of her eyes to stave off tears. "Cassidy? A minute, please?"

Two of Leda's assistants were gliding in to prepare the dressing rooms for the rest of the bridesmaids' fittings. Garment bags boasting the ladies' names had been hung on the doors. The woman named Cassidy passed her task to another associate and came forth to help record measurements.

By the time they were finished, the entire entourage had gravitated to the suite. Drinks were going around again, and since only a couple of people could indulge in the luxurious perfection of the champagne, Joey sneaked another glass when Tem was occupied by conversation.

"Is it delicious?" Danica Blue asked, perhaps noticing Joey's almost-orgasmic reaction to the champagne.

"Uh-huh. Get a glass. Flutes are still going around."

"Actually—" Danica hesitated, then smoothed her wispy bangs and started slinking toward the dressing rooms. "Never mind. I think I saw someone come through with my dress. Better get this measurement out of the way."

"Okay." Joey went to her own dressing room and found it stocked with a basket of sewing instruments, a wide stepstool and a vase full of fat apricot-and-cream roses.

It was all so pristinely elegant that she was overly careful with each movement so as not to mar or damage anything as she stripped to her undies.

A knock on the door made her yelp.

"Miss de la Peña, do you need any help?" someone called through the door.

"Nope, I can manage." Getting dressed every day wasn't a dramatic event, so long as she kept all articles within reach and didn't have to walk more than a few steps. Her damaged hip couldn't bear much weight and when it locked up, motion was impossible. "Just step in, right?"

"Right. Press the little call button near the top of the stall door when you're ready to be zipped."

Joey opened the garment bag and sighed. The gown, deep lavender with a strapless beaded bodice and a flared lace-over-silk skirt, was fit for the type of princess who'd ditch the ball and sneak off into the night with a man too devilish and sexy to be considered a princely hero.

"Lottie, you know me too well, don't you?" When she stepped into the gown and faced the mirror, she almost cried. A decent tan, proper underthings and accessories would complete the transformation, but already she was convinced that Leda J. Dawson was more of a fairy godmother than a gown-designing bridal consultant.

"Ow—damn it!"

Joey's head cocked in the direction of the outburst. She didn't hear any knocks on the neighboring stall doors and listened to the silence closely for muffled sounds.

"Ow, ow, ow!"

"Uh, hello?" she called, holding the dress up with one

hand and grabbing her cane with the other. The voice came from the next stall.

"Joey?"

"Danica, you're still trying on your dress?"

"Yes." Radio silence. "Ma's going to be pissed."

Uh-oh. This didn't sound encouraging.

"Want a stepstool chat?"

"Yeah."

Joey carefully got on her stool and made it to the second tier before she was able to comfortably see over the top of the stall. Danica was already there, her arms folded on top of the partition. "What's the matter?"

"The bodice of my dress is too snug."

"Isn't that how it was designed? All of the other—"

"And my nipples are sore."

"Uh…" Joey said again, frowning. Danica had avoided champagne, and now she was complaining of a too-snug dress and sore nipples? "Danni, are you *pregnant*?"

"A little. I mean, yes, pregnant. Not very far along."

"*Ay, Dios mio*… This has got to be the most fertile wedding in Las Vegas's history. I'm going to research that." She realized something else. "I'm the only woman in Lottie's entourage who isn't pregnant."

"My sister said you're dating someone."

"Affirmative."

"Well, regular sex has its benefits, but you might want to double down on the protection if you want to remain the only woman in Charlotte's entourage who's not pregnant. Dex and I use condoms every time and here I am two months along."

They were also having unusually copious amounts of sex, according to Blue family gossip. Since condoms were said to be only ninety-something percent effective, the odds of dodging a surprise probably weren't exactly in their favor.

"Does your man know you're preggers?"

Danica nodded emphatically. "I told him right away. He was as stunned as I was, because we hadn't planned for this, but he was happy. Really happy. Five minutes later we were celebrating."

Joey tried to hold back her side-eye. She failed. At least Danica couldn't get pregnant while *already* pregnant. "If you think he's happy now, just wait until you guys discover no-condom sex."

Danica surrendered to a crinkly-eyed smile. "We already have, and it's *amazing*."

Okay, then. "For someone with such exceptional control on the football field, Dex sure can't hang on to his self-control with you."

"I wouldn't have it any other way. We're in love."

Love was good to Danica and Dex. Even as she reminded herself that she didn't want what they had because love required too much risk, she envied their ability to take the risk and to trust what they felt for each other.

"It's obvious you haven't told Tem. Why not?"

"This is the third alteration to my dress. This time she's going to notice that only the bust needs to be let out, and, come on, that's a glaring indicator."

"Danica, I meant, if you and Dex are completely over the moon, why haven't you shared the baby news with your parents?"

"We wouldn't dream of overshadowing Charlotte's wedding. She's brave enough to allow Ma to have such influence over all of this, so she deserves the glory of a perfect day. Which she will have, providing neither Krissy nor Martha goes into early labor. God forbid."

Joey echoed the sentiment in Spanish, adding a blessing.

"Also," Danica said, almost timidly, "he and I want this for ourselves. We want time for privacy, time to enjoy being together before everyone else—family and the NFL and the media—get involved. I'm not explaining myself clearly, am I?"

"I think I understand, though, Danica. Will you and Mr. Quarterback be squeezing in a vacation before the season starts?"

"We're thinking something more meaningful than that. We want to be married, before the season begins, and the fewer people who know about it, the better."

Uh-oh again. "Why are you telling me?"

"Why *not* tell you?" Danica shook her head. "Joey, you're who I need in my corner for this. My best friend's mother operates a matchmaking business. Veda would never keep this secret from Willa. Dex's agent has agreed to stand up for him and I need you to stand up for me." Danica gripped the partition. "Please, Joey? Who can keep things confidential better than a sports agent and an ex-FBI agent?"

"So I'm a chosen one because I can hold a secret?"

"You have a good heart, Joey. You're a sweet person even if you try not to be. And to be completely forthcoming and selfish on top of it, I need your help arranging a court-house ceremony. We need this under wraps."

"Are you sure, Danica? To be married in secret and have no one congratulate you on being newlyweds?"

"We don't need that. We have each other, we have love, and eventually…" She glanced down toward her tummy, and her smile could melt a million hearts.

Joey blurted, "Okay. I'm saying yes."

"You'll help us?"

"I will."

"Aww, thank you!" Danica's eyes turned misty and she fanned her face. "Oh, God. It's hormones. I'd better get out there. Let's talk more later. I can't wait to tell Dex to-night. He'll be so happy."

So happy that he'd take Danica aside and they would *celebrate*, which was as per their usual?

"Then I should expect your call sometime tomorrow when you and your man *aren't* within groping distance of each other?"

Danica laughed. "Fine. Tomorrow. Judge us now, but wait until you're in love. Sex is great when it's a casual thing, but once you mix love into it…boom."

Descending the stool slowly, and hearing Danica leave her stall and walk down the hall that led to the suite's main room, Joey figured she was in no position to judge. She and Zaf weren't in a loving relationship yet he had left her exhausted and well-done every day since she'd given him her key. Not to mention they were guilty of multiple counts of dirty public foreplay.

She wasn't sorry for any of it. She hurt because he'd never loved her, was confused because he behaved as though he *did* love her, was angry that he kept himself shrouded in secrecy, but she wouldn't erase any second of being body-to-body with him.

She cherished the moments he was with her and inside her and close enough to make her feel safe.

That was the strangeness in this. He made her feel protected, yet she couldn't trust him—especially not after what she'd learned this morning. The methods he'd used to get the information he wanted from Alessandro Franco were ripped from Archangel's playbook.

I'm not him. I'm not that other guy.

God help her, she did trust that. If she didn't, he wouldn't still have access to her house or her life.

Joey considered her reflection again. Her shoes hadn't yet been finalized, but the gown could stand to lose a half inch or so. She was certain the LJD staff would find plenty of imperfections she missed, and she was too in love with the garment to want to criticize it.

A tap on the door came, and this time she was ready to be zipped. "Come in. It's beautiful—"

"Sono d'accordo con te."

Gian DiGorgio moved easily, calmly, shutting the dressing room door behind him and engaging the lock. His raven-black suit stood out like priceless ink spilled against the eggshell-colored walls. His face was jagged, unrefined stone—hard and threatening against the soft pastel environment.

His expensive scent choked her, and the compassionless hatred in his eyes stung.

He took a step forward and she made the civilian mistake of retreating *away* from anything she could use to defend herself.

Her weight rested on her strong leg, but the position wouldn't sustain her much longer. For a dressing room, this one was spacious—and while ordinarily that'd be a luxury she appreciated, right now it sucked major ass. The center of the room was open to accommodate extravagant dresses and multiple people fussing over this and that. She couldn't get to a wall without hopping an awkward distance or attempting to shift her weight to a weak hip that wouldn't hold up.

So she stayed where she stood, cataloging the creases and beard pattern and unique characteristics of his face as her periphery monitored his hands.

Reach for a weapon, any weapon, you bastard, and I'll find a way to disable you.

"Where are my friends?"

"Undisturbed in that outer room, *belladonna*. You wouldn't accuse me of threatening them, would you?"

"You're here uninvited, just as you were at the Slayers' training camp the other day. Now you're in my changing room with the door locked, and I don't want you here. So, in case this is unclear to you, Gian, I want you to get the hell out."

"I see." The man nodded deeply. "You don't like people poking around where they don't belong."

She didn't answer. She knew where he was going with this and wouldn't entertain him. Her mind stubbornly wanted to panic, but she tried to think clearly. She had been trained for moments like this, had encountered full-on violent attacks and managed to survive them all.

There were no cameras in the dressing rooms. There was an emergency exit nearby—was that how he'd gained entry?

"What you did, Josephine, was stir up some…inconveniences. You interfered with my business operations. You compromised me. You damaged my profits. You bloodied my reputation—"

"I revealed your crimes. A genius is what you are, right? For a genius, you did a crappy job of covering your tracks. Blame yourself. Intimidate yourself." Provoking a cold and illogical criminal with an ax to grind ranked high on the foolish scale, but she was furious that this man bathed her in fear.

"*Puttana*. A man should put you in your place."

Joey resisted gritting her teeth. She had views about men who thought women needed to be put in their place. A few branches of her family tree presented households functioning on a "me-man, you-woman, man-rules-woman" model that burned her bacon. "It won't be you."

"Confident about that?"

"Outsourcing everything keeps your hands clean, true, but it shows what a weak, no-balls coward you really are."

The insult struck him, crackling in his faded blue eyes, and he took a single step toward her. Closer and she could connect, fist to face.

Although physical confrontations weren't her preferred

method of getting a point across, she was capable of defending herself.

"I don't outsource everything." Gian raised a hand, but ran it down his crisply cut silver hair. "Your house is full of life. Bright. Welcoming. But you do own an alarming amount of clothes. Vanity is a vice, isn't it?"

Joey's throat felt tight. "Bastard. You *were* in my house."

Gian watched her a moment, and she hated the slide of his gaze down her body. She held the dress tighter to her chest. "Anytime, Josephine. Anytime that I want to get to you, I will. I will use my hands and I will make you curse the day you interfered with my casino. The law can't protect you. Neither can your man. He's not here, but I am."

He took yet another step, but not toward her. He picked up her cane and tossed it over the partition then unlocked her stall and walked smoothly out.

Joey started to shiver and she hated that. Weakness, vulnerability, inadequacy—it all began pushing to the surface. Why had she let down her guard, even for a moment, and allowed Gian DiGorgio to catch her unprotected? Why hadn't she kept a weapon strapped to her thigh? Why had she set her cane down, when she couldn't move without it?

She tried to get to the call button next to the stall door. Two steps forward and she spilled onto the floor.

Damn it!

She reached to grip the edge of a table, but ended up catching a sheer cloth and yanking down everything that had been arranged on top of it. The vase broke into large chunks and the roses...

The roses bounced and quivered and lay in a puddle of water.

And she started to cry.

When someone shouted her name, she didn't know how many minutes had passed.

"Miss de la Peña, I am *so* sorry! The door was locked,

if you can believe it. It locks from the inside to protect our clients' items, but the emergency door was locked, too. It's the strangest thing. No one locks the dressing entry during salon hours. We can't find the key. Oh, Lord, what happened to you?"

Joey sniffled and saw Leda, Charlotte and Tem and an assistant barreling into the stall. "I fell."

"Oh, your dress," Tem said. "It's wet."

"Ma, I'm more concerned about her than I am about the damn dress," Charlotte said tersely. "Would you please unlock that outer door and let everyone know we've had an incident?"

Tem did an about-face, murmuring coolly to her daughter, "Watch your tone. Grow up, get married, but I'm still your mother."

Charlotte accepted Leda's profuse apologies on Joey's behalf, stepped beside her and lowered to her haunches. "You fell?"

Joey looked at her, shaking her head.

"How in the world did your cane end up in the next changing room?" Leda asked incredulously when her assistant returned to the dressing room holding the stick.

"Can I have a sec with her?" Charlotte asked as the assistant began to clean up the broken glass. When they stepped away, she said, "That son of a bitch was here, wasn't he? What did he do?"

"Intimidated me, took my cane away. I *had* the bastard, Lottie. I had him red-effing-handed and he walked away without any of you knowing he was here to begin with. If he'd hurt any of you..."

"We are fine. It's you I'm worried about. Let me call Nate. Gian's his godfather. He needs to be aware of this, Joey."

"No. It's the reaction he wants. He wants to know that

he can frighten me. He confronted me full-on today. I don't think it'll be long before he makes a real move."

"I'm scared for you," her friend said firmly. "Maybe this is something you're used to, but I'm not. Go to the police. Please."

"He's walked away a free man once. It'll happen again, Lottie."

"Then where is Zaf? He's supposed to protect you."

"We had a fight this morning and I asked him to not come here or to the dinner."

"Call him."

"I—" Joey sobbed, sniffled then reached to start picking up the roses. "I can't."

"Then I will." Charlotte rooted around in Joey's purse, didn't comment on the weapon she must've encountered, and pulled out the phone. "Zaf, this is Charlotte Blue. I'm at LJD's Couture Brides. Joey needs you."

Joey and Charlotte remained in the dressing room, seated on the floor saying nothing as staff came in to clean the mess and Tem poked her head in to report she'd sent everyone else ahead to Le Cirque.

Leda's voice had them both looking up. "Ladies, again, I'm so sorry. None of the staff knows where the key could've gone. It grew legs and ran off."

"Cassidy," Joey said. The woman hadn't appeared in the dressing rooms area when the commotion hit. "Where is she?"

"She went home sick— Wait. I'm certain there's a sensible explanation."

Sure there is. It's green paper and has the power to buy and sell people.

Zaf arrived and went directly to Joey, crouching and scooping her into his arms, then carrying her in a trail of lavender silk to a settee.

Faintly she was aware of Charlotte and Leda both sighing, "Oh."

Joey hugged him. "You smell like sawdust. Were you working on the shoe closet? Even though we argued?"

"You're building her a shoe closet?" Leda asked with a taken little smile. "You are a prince."

He wasn't, though. He was the flawed, dangerous, devilish man she wanted.

"About earlier," she began, feeling the need to put into words that despite what they'd said before, she did need him now. She wanted him to stay with her.

"It's okay," he said against her temple.

It wasn't, but if she held on tight enough and believed hard enough, maybe it would be.

Joey had tears on her cheeks when she fell asleep—and Zaf was ready to cause some pain. Slipping out of the house at the height of night, he drove to DiGorgio Royal Casino.

Gian DiGorgio was a defiant son of a bitch, continuing to operate the casino while it was for sale and remaining a fixture at the place even as it bled investors and its clientele.

Zaf figured it came in handy now. The vacantness made DiGorgio easy to locate.

In the Mahogany Lounge, the silver-haired sociopath commanded a table decorated with liquor, cigars and playing cards.

"It took you longer to get here than I expected," the man said, not looking up when Zaf approached his table. "Her fear finally lured you from your hidey-hole."

"You don't know me."

"I've been hoping to change that fact. First, I wondered if you were a legend—a phantom. Now I see you're a mortal man, with weaknesses." DiGorgio plucked the cigar from his mouth, and the wet end glistened under the lounge's gold lights. With a slow, slurred blend of Italian and English, he dismissed the people gathered at the table for a lazy hand of poker. "Sit down, Zaf. Take a cigar. Here's a light."

Zaf claimed a seat, eyed the older man steadily as he lit the cigar and took a deep drag.

"You and Josephine," DiGorgio said. "You deserve each other. Both of you have an annoying way of involving yourselves in other people's affairs."

"Target her and you target me. Is that what you want?"

"She's too by-the-book to be more than a nuisance to me," DiGorgio decided. "She'll follow the law off a short pier. But that's her flaw. You, Zaf Ahmadi—Archangel—you crossed lines that folks don't cross if they love their lives." He started sweeping his hands over the table to gather cards. "When did you stop loving your life? In lockup? The military? After the first kill…the tenth…the fiftieth?"

Zaf didn't allow a single muscle to twitch in response.

"Keep smoking. That's a quality cigar. I don't want to see it go to waste." DiGorgio was glowering now as he scanned the nearly empty lounge. Business had gone to shit—that was what hurt him below the belt. "Wilcox was one of yours, wasn't he? Tell me the truth and you walk out of here the way you came. Lie and I can't guarantee that you won't end up spilled in an alley."

"I hired Wilcox to intercept the order you put out on Al Franco. That's why Franco's still alive. By the way, I don't feel threats. They bounce off the armor."

"Hmm. But you're here confronting me in my establishment after I had a friendly chat with your woman, so evidently you feel something." DiGorgio sat back, sighed. "Too many men fall because of some irrational attachment to a woman. Women are among the world's most plentiful commodities. Easy acquisitions, and they all have a price."

"Wrong, but feel free to continue rambling like the crazy old bastard that you are." Zaf had an innocuous smile ready, and he could tell the lid on the other man's temper was beginning to tremble.

"My question remains unanswered. When did you stop loving your life? Was it—" DiGorgio rested his hands flat on the table "—when your cousin got himself quartered in DC eight years ago?"

Zaf kept his form relaxed until the moment that he was up and had the other man contorted against the wall before his chair crashed to the floor.

DiGorgio's face began to redden, but he grunted out, "The FBI wanted you only because you're a ticking time bomb they'd rather have on their side than against it. Your woman, Josephine—do you genuinely believe she can forgive you for crippling her?"

The question threw Zaf, causing him to loosen his hold.

"This is my offer, Zaf Ahmadi. It expires in exactly one minute. Work for me. Give me your loyalty and let the woman go. Perhaps, if you prove yourself loyal and capable during a probationary period, I'll get you what you need for retribution for that stupid kid cousin of yours."

"I don't need the minute," Zaf said. "To hell with your offer."

"As I said, too many men fall. Woman will always be the demise of man."

Zaf released him, though not before immobilizing him and letting him drop. "Come near Josephine again, scare her again, and I will hunt you."

DiGorgio coughed, angrily watching him. "You shouldn't have come here. Love made you do that, didn't it? That was the worst mistake you'll make."

There were a few things the old man could do with his threats, but Zaf strode out of the Mahogany Lounge and

DiGorgio Royal Casino with his adrenaline rushing and his heart beating wildly until he was back at Joey's house.

She was still asleep in her bedroom. Zaf stood in the doorway for a few moments, observing her through the dark. What the hell could he do for her now? DiGorgio wasn't going to let her go, and Zaf couldn't.

Was he the best man to shield her when he loved her to complete desperation?

Go to your room. Go to sleep. Leave her alone.

But that was the problem—he was incapable of leaving her alone.

There were plenty of reasons that would justify walking away.

She was angry with him.

She didn't know if she could forgive his handling of Alessandro Franco's confession in Italy.

She didn't know the secrets he kept.

She didn't know he loved her.

Zaf rejected the part of him that warned he should allow some distance. Selfishly, he came nearer just to touch her soft, soft skin and reassure himself that tonight she hadn't been taken from him.

"Zaf," she said on a drowsy sigh, wrapped around one of her pillows. She released the pillow and caught his shirt. "Come here."

He toed off his shoes and slid onto the bed, and she automatically draped an arm around him.

"I felt it, when you left the bed. Where'd you go?"

"Go back to sleep, Jo."

She snuggled against him. "What did you smoke?"

"A cigar. You probably don't want to kiss me, then."

Joey's mouth found his in the dark. "I don't care about that tonight. Kiss me, okay?" After he complied—thoroughly— she said, "You taste like Jelly Belly."

"I ate a handful when I came home. I think I'm eating more than you are."

"Good thing you bought the big jar." She paused, gently working a hand underneath his shirt to stroke his chest. "Hey. You said *home*."

This place was the first that'd felt like home in a long time. The words refused to form, however.

Joey yawned, but began to pull up his shirt to lay kisses across his abs. He knew her body was tired. "I want to go home, to my real home."

"Your family reunion's around the corner." She would be safest with her family right now, but he wasn't in the position to reveal to her how he could be so certain of that.

"Come with me. I want you to meet the family. They'll like you."

"Go back to sleep," he whispered. "I'll go to the reunion with you."

"When it comes down to it with DiGorgio, I'm going to face him alone."

"I won't leave you alone."

"It's not that I'm all that afraid anymore—about that," she continued as though he hadn't spoken. "What scares me is that something will happen and you won't know that I—" Joey suddenly stopped, took her hand from his chest and turned her backside to him. "I guess I am really wiped."

Had she been on the verge of saying *love*? Did she love him despite every reason she shouldn't?

Zaf's fingers found her waist, drifted somehow to encounter the knotted terrain of her scar. "Josephine... God, Jo, I love you."

The whisper of her even breathing was the response he got. It was just as well. Complicated confessions, words he had no right to say, belonged unanswered in the dark.

Chapter 10

"June Creek's about a half hour outside the city," Joey said from the passenger seat of a rented Ford F-350 Crew Cab. El Paso International Airport was far behind them but there was a ways to go before she and Zaf would drive beneath the wood-and-metal Yellow Hawk Ranch sign. The open road carved into the desert landscape, presenting an opportunity to lower the window, take off her aviator sunglasses and consume the sights, sounds and scents of the familiar stranger that would always be home to her. But almost of its own defiance, her body was tuned into Zaf. A seat belt was the only thing keeping her from crawling to his lap and curling up there.

Zaf reached to squeeze her thigh, and she applauded herself for wearing a pair of short-shorts with her camisole. His hand rested there, where it belonged. She skated her fingers over the fine dark hair along his forearm, traced his large knuckles, toyed with the watch and the beads and the straps on his wrist.

"Our spread's at the farthest edge of town, traveling this route. We should be at the ranch before dark, but there are two stops I need to make before we get there."

The first was to The Flannel Blanket—or, as locals called it, Blanket's. When Joey had been a kid, the folks running the massive Western apparel store held the glass door with a lawn gnome, the town's ugliest doorstop. The autumn she and her friend had worked the closing shift to wage-earn their way to a ski trip up north, they'd decided—with encouragement from too much rum-spiced cider—that it would be funny to dress the gnome up as Santa Claus. Drawing on spectacles and rosy red cheeks with Magic Markers, they had come into work the next day to news that they'd been fired and fined for defacing a valuable town artifact.

Automatic sliders had replaced the old glass door and gnome. Stepping inside with Zaf, she wondered if the store owners had forgotten the hell she and Honey Sutherland had raised in their heyday, all in the grand scheme of being a couple of bored country girls sowing some wild oats.

Probably not, seeing as Jacob and Coraline Sutherland had been the ones handing down the punishments for one half of the teenage troublemaking duo.

"I'm looking for something specific," she told Zaf as they passed a row of snakeskin belts and a table topped with leather wallets and shaving kit cases. "Have a look around. I worked here once—ran the counter, stocked inventory. Sometimes, off the clock, I helped the entertainment sound check." She looked toward the other side of the store and found a modest wood stage set up and a chalkboard where the performers' names were always posted. "Looks like nobody's scheduled for the weekend. Are you still any good on the acoustic?"

"Don't think about it," he interrupted. "I'm in cowboy country, but there are two things I won't do while we're here. Play the guitar and wear a hat."

"Boo," she teased, and damn, did it feel incredible to joke around and know a sense of safety, no matter how fragile it was.

"You sang a song in Spanish at the bar in Mexico that first night," he commented, taking her back to those moments that had been charged with sexual awareness and unexplainable need. "So many sides to you, Jo. All of them made to hook me."

She stilled her cane and grabbed hold of him by his buckle. "I'm glad you're here. If work hadn't kept us in DC or out on jobs, would you have brought me home to your folks in Jersey?"

"No, because I haven't been back in eight years."

"Your parents are likely missing you."

"They don't know who I am anymore," he said softly. "I don't think I do, either."

I know who you are. I know I'm in love with you.

But they were friends with benefits because that was all of himself he would give her. As she habitually did, Joey accepted what she could get. "I'm checking out the boots. My mother's side would be offended to know I brought sneakers and stilettos but not a single pair of boots."

Mulling over the selections, she decided on a sandy-brown pair with turquoise embroidery and cherry leather inlay. Then, craning her neck to get a visual on Zaf, who was in conversation with the person behind the counter, she joined the shoppers fussing over the impressive collection of hats.

Determined to get him to do both of the things he said he wouldn't on this trip, she started by choosing a black Stetson and hauling her finds to the counter.

"I'm not wearing that," he said, setting her boots on the counter.

"No?" She motioned for him to lean so she could whisper in his ear, "Wear this hat and I'll do you in the back of the truck."

Zaf slid the Stetson toward the register. "Do you accept American Express?"

Joey was wicked and not an ounce sorry for it. She would make good on the deal, some night this week after dark when the stars came out of hiding.

"Josephine de la Peña?" the woman behind the counter asked, already rushing around the counter.

"Hi, Coraline." She braced herself for a sympathetic look but instead got a hearty hug. "This is my boyfriend, Zaf. So, where's the hometown girl?" she asked when Coraline returned to the register.

"Delivering one of her orders. She teaches art at the elementary school, but during the summers you can hardly take her attention off her stained glass studio. Are you heading to Yellow Hawk?"

"After I see Papá at the shop."

"Okay. I'll let Honey know you're back. Don't y'all start cutting up and painting the town red the way you used to."

"Can't promise that," Joey said with an angelic smile.

"Trouble, both of you. Oh, hey, Josephine—" Coraline waited until Zaf was out the sliding doors before she said conspiratorially, "Don't tell my husband I said this, but your man is oh, my God, hot!"

Their next stop was Bonita Gardens of Texas. It wasn't until they'd parked in the lot that she finally confided that she'd spoken with her father the day before and he wanted a man-to-man talk with Zaf.

"Papá's traditional," she told him. "He's protective of me. We can't exactly hold him at fault for being cautious."

"Is he going to be waiting with a shotgun at the ready or something?"

"Only if he's cleaning it." She tried not to alarm him, but getting past her father's reservations would be only the first obstacle. It was her mother, Anita, Zaf would need to approach with utmost care. The gentle-voiced accountant with the big brown eyes and dimpled smile had an intricate personality. Not many knew exactly how intricate.

"Do they know about Arizona?" he asked.

"Some secrets are mine to keep, even from the family. I never told them you were the shooter. All they know is you're in law enforcement and we're dating." She gently added, "Both of my parents are willing to trust my judgment. But since we expect a full house at the ranch, Mamá and Papá want to establish that you have gentlemanly intentions."

Zaf looked her dead in the eyes. "I certainly do not. In fact…"

His filthy words left a blush on her cheeks that remained as they entered the main building.

While Blanket's renovations were no more dramatic than new doors and a fresh coat of paint, the town's family-owned florist had undergone a transformation that included increased square footage, a second-story addition that held offices and a consultation room, and delivery vans that looked more like showroom SUVs that boasted the company logo.

"Is Hector de la Peña around?" she asked the receptionist. "I'm his daughter, Joey."

"Oh, hello! You're today's top subject. He's in the greenhouse. Go have a seat in the consult room, and I'll page him."

When Hector arrived, he promptly reintroduced Joey to the hall and shut the door, leaving her blisteringly indignant as she paced and looked through the glass wall and tried pitifully to gauge their conversation.

But she'd been privy to none of it. When Hector finally swaggered to the door and opened it, she stepped in and said, "*¡Válgame Dios!* Papá, if I didn't miss you so much, I would be pissed that you did this. I'm not a little girl. You can't grill my boyfriends."

"Zaf's a good man, *mija*," Hector declared, deflating her fury. "Take him home to meet the family."

Joey hugged her father, staring over his shoulder at Zaf. "What did you say?" she mouthed.

Zaf put his palms together and bowed his head as if to say, "I was a saint."

When they reached Yellow Hawk Ranch, the sun was sitting low and the main house brimmed with people. Most of the family had arrived yesterday, so she and Zaf were late arrivals. If that wasn't enough to call too much attention to them, Joey's cane picked up any slack. Relatives converged from every direction, pulling her into conversations that put her bilingual ability to good use.

Somehow she and Zaf got separated. The Yellow Hawk Ranch sat on several acres of open Texas land, the closest neighbor was over a mile away…but for the first time in days she felt at peace without needing to have him in her sight.

"I want to know what you said to Zaf," she warned Hector once he'd returned to a house all but vibrating with noise and music and life.

"*Sí*, okay. We'll talk in the garden, after I help you and Anita here." He came to his wife, nuzzling her neck and murmuring something that might be romantic if Hector and Anita weren't *her parents*.

"Eh, *cochino*. No foreplay over the food," someone ribbed.

She and her mother ruled the rustic millionaire-meets-mountain-living kitchen, selecting lemons for what must be the third pitcher of fresh-made lemonade of the afternoon. Liquor was plentiful—and going fast—but there were more underage cousins than Joey had realized, and they were a thirsty, demanding lot.

"Hurry up!" five-year-old Graciela shouted. "If I stay thirsty for too long, I get hiccups. When I get hiccups, I have to drink more to stop the hiccups. When I drink more, I pee in my jammies. When I pee in my jammies, Mommy gets mad."

"Gracie, *vamanos*," Joey's brother, Eduardo, said, swooping in to interrupt the onset of a preschool diva's tantrum.

He looked like a normal kid guilty of following trends—tattoos on his arm, which Anita had called her to commiserate over, and the sides of his head shaved low with the rest of his hair in a man-bun that might be kind of edgy hot to the girls around town.

Only, Eddie was following a path that Joey found familiar. At seventeen, Eddie had his eye on law studies and his ambitions set on Quantico.

"*Gracias*," Joey said, waving them over. "But she reminds me of you at that age, Eddie. Impatient, petulant—"

"What's pech-u-ant mean?" Graciela asked.

"Josephine means to say you're being a brat," Anita explained, handing the girl a plastic cup. "Of course, who knows a brat better than a brat?"

Joey scrunched her face. "How *could* you say I'm a brat? I was thinking I'm your favorite."

"You're my favorite daughter." Anita laughed at Joey's "Hey!" Passing off her lemon-squeezing duties to her husband, she said, "Josephine, your father said you'd called some time ago and asked for me. Is there something going on that I should know about?"

"No, Mamá." *Lies.* "I'm just here for family."

Over an hour had passed before she was able to slip away from the chaos and meet Hector in the garden, which was actually an eco-friendly greenhouse where he often spent time to reflect.

Joey shut the door, and there was a weighty silence that

seemed louder than the hum of the cooling system. "You worry about me too much, Papá."

"I can't help it. I don't care that you're an adult and you're smart and you work in law enforcement. None of that matters to me because you're my daughter."

"Is the cane hard to look at?"

"No, it's the fear in your eyes. Tell me what's scaring you."

She couldn't. At some point she'd thought that she might be able to, but with so much family here—in the house, visiting the stables, playing rowdy card games in the carriage house—she didn't want to wreck the reunion.

For their sake, she swallowed her childish instinct to run to her parents, who'd slay her dragons then do everything to map out the rest of her life.

She would show them she could take care of herself, even if she had to lie.

"I'm not scared," she told her father. "I'm just nervous that you and Mamá might mistreat my boyfriend."

"Zaf. Has Anita taken a look at him?"

"Beyond shaking his hand and telling him to eat plenty? No, and she won't. When I was a teenager she promised she wouldn't pry. My relationships are my business."

"She wants to protect you."

"Papá, I've heard this all before. Corpus Christi happened over twenty years ago, and I've been through a lot—with Zaf."

"He cares about you. It's what we talked about at the flower shop."

"I know." *But he doesn't love me.* "Can I ask you, how do you sleep in the same bed as Mamá and work with her and love her, knowing in your heart that there will always be secrets?"

"Anita's the love of my life."

"What about Eddie and me? Papá, I have to tell you... I passed the LSATs."

Hector ruffled his gray-streaked hair, crossed his arms and turned toward a row of cacti. "Yeah. You were too intelligent to fail, but too concerned about my ego to defy me. Why tell me now?"

"To ask you how you can go on loving me when there are lies and secrets. Your daughter chose the FBI over the flower shop. Eddie's speed-racing down that same road."

"Josephine, I love my family. It's as simple as that. As the head of this household, I can exercise certain power, but ultimately you have your own minds. Whatever I can't control, I address in prayer. It's all I can do."

A few taps on the greenhouse door preceded a woman with short blond waves and downturned blue eyes. "So you went away and came back the ultimate hottie."

"Honey!" Joey pushed her cane to its limit and it jabbed the ground ferociously as she hurried to her childhood bestie. She heard her father mutter something about avoiding girl gossip as he left the greenhouse. "Coraline said you were working today."

"At my studio, yes. But I make my own hours, so I'm here." Honey squeezed her hand. "Let's split."

"And go where? It's dark now."

"All the sexy cowboys hit Dusty's after dark."

"I'm not in the market. I have a man."

"Yay for you, darlin'. But I'm currently between men— and not in the good way. For old times' sake, come with. Go put on something that says 'I live in Las Vegas so you better impress me.'"

They were Joey and Honey, the naughty gals of June Creek, Texas, again. Joey didn't pass up the chance to rediscover this part of herself. At the main house she changed into a short pleated dress and her new boots and was taking the rear stairs when her brother caught her.

"Sneaking out?"

"Yes. Honey Sutherland's waiting outside and we're going to Dusty's."

"What about your dude?"

"Zaf's from our world, Eddie. I'm sure he can handle the family on his own."

His face changed. "Yeah. Birds of a feather work together."

"Ed—"

"Screw it. Forget I said that. What lie do you want me give Mamá and Papá when they ask where you went?"

"Don't lie. Just wait ten minutes before you snitch. I don't want the family ganging up on me to guilt me *and* Honey into staying put."

"Fine. You're supposed to be the responsible older sibling, you know."

"Who the hell said that?"

Eddie smiled. "Know something? If you hung around more often, I wouldn't be off-my-ass shocked that you're actually kind of cool."

This part of the de la Peñas' main house was quiet—or what passed for quiet in a place packed with people talking, hollering at TV sports, singing along to music and jiving around.

Coming into a parlor that resembled Joey's offbeat decorating style but with unmistakably high-end flair, Zaf gratefully accepted the drink a housekeeper brewed from an espresso machine on the buffet near the door.

He didn't speak until he'd sunk his weary body onto a slipcovered parsons chair, drank through the burn of the liquid and rubbed his eyes. "I think you chose the wrong man for this assignment."

Anita Esposito de la Peña, halfway up a rolling ladder

with a stack of books in the crook of one arm, stopped what she was doing and climbed down.

She'd given Joey her petite frame and dainty air that folks would think was more suited for storybook fairies than federal agents. The difference was Anita harbored no doubts. The FBI had been her stepping-stone; the elite covert securities branch she ran with her uncles and brother was her lifeblood.

"A cup of what he's drinking, Yasmin?" she asked the housekeeper, her smile as fresh as the bouquets he'd seen creatively arranged in Bonita Gardens' lobby. The woman balanced dual lives masterfully. The Anita who June Creek knew was a pillar of a small community, a florist's wife, an accountant and an attentive mother. The Anita *he* knew was a flinty, unshakable ex-agent who helped run an underground security firm and wasn't afraid to grab a guy by the balls to get things done.

Merge the two and she was an almost superhumanly fascinating individual.

"I'm requesting to be taken off the job, Anita." He continued to speak freely—as Yasmin wasn't a housekeeper at all. She was an operative installed within the household while Anita groomed her as an assistant, and was currently helping Eduardo de la Peña develop intelligence techniques.

The assistant who'd trained Joey to hone her memorization and face-cataloging skills when she was a child had been assigned the role of equestrian groomer and years ago quietly left the industry to enjoy a tropical retirement in Barbados.

Anita and her children had been conditioned for the most dangerous recesses of law enforcement. Hector de la Peña was an average scientist running an average florist company. God help the man.

"*Que pasa?* Around here a man's word is all he has,"

Anita began, setting the books down on a table before sitting cross-legged on the floor and taking her espresso. "You gave me and my firm your word that you'd see this to the end."

"I should've told you no in the beginning," he said, recalling how it had nearly crumbled him that Joey's mother had personally sought him out and pulled him out of the shadows because she'd learned Gian DiGorgio was tracking her daughter. Zaf's reunion with Joey had been months in the making, carefully planned to the finest detail so he could be reinserted into her life and act as her shield until DiGorgio could be convicted and neutralized. "I shouldn't have let the past and my goddamn guilt rope me in."

"But…" she said gently, "that's not what roped you in. There's no question you felt horrible after hurting her in Arizona. To shoot the woman you loved while trying to rescue her? Awful."

"I didn't take this assignment because I need the money. In fact, don't pay me. Not a cent. I won't take it."

Anita exchanged a smirk with Yasmin, who strutted to gather the books and shelve them.

"What was that about?" he demanded.

"I owe Yasmin a hundred dollars."

"For?"

"She's a wagering woman. Really, it's a sickness. Anyway, she said you would try to quit. I said you'd stand by our simple terms." Anita stared into her cup. "I still intend to connect you with the pigs who took your cousin. He was hardly older than my son when he died. You should know I pray for his soul—yours, as well."

"Thank you, Anita, but I can't effectively guard Joey. Tonight she left the ranch—"

"Yes, mmm-hmm, I'm aware. Honey Sutherland helped her escape to a bar."

The woman didn't appear concerned. "Is Honey—"

"A part of the business? No. However, she was an annoyingly inquisitive child. When the girls were twelve, they conspired by email to meet an out-of-towner, and I intervened before it came to that. For three years Honey pestered my husband and me, because she couldn't fathom how we knew every detail of their silly plan." Anita drank then started to twirl her curly brown hair. "It came to a head at Joey's Quinceañera. The girls were going to sneak to El Paso, I blocked them and it came out that I'd been hacking Joey's email. She was *pissed* and had me swear to never spy on her again. Honey, however, was intrigued. She's not on my payroll, but that may change. She's loyal to the family. Loyalty is very valuable."

"DiGorgio got close to Joey. It rattled her and it almost pushed me too far."

"Did you use a weapon?"

"No."

"You did the right thing, Zaf. Gian DiGorgio isn't hiding or sending minions to handle the messy work. That's a good thing, though it can't seem that way now."

"Anita, he got to her because Joey asked me to stay away and I respected that. My job is to keep her safe, but it's as if I'm less of a bodyguard and more of a... Damn it."

Joey's mother had the gall to smile. "More of a lover?"

Zaf and Yasmin looked at her, speechless.

"Are we not all adults in this room? Zaf, you and I are engaging in an adult conversation. Yasmin, you're openly eavesdropping on an adult conversation." She set her cup aside. "Zafir Ahmadi, you're the one my daughter chose. While she's parading you around as her boyfriend and while she *believes* Hector and I don't already know the danger she's in, I see that there's more truth to your 'fake' relationship than either of you will admit."

"Yeah?"

"You love Josephine."

Yasmin was no longer shelving books, but was up high on the rolling ladder and smiling against a handful of hard-covers. "You love the hell out of her."

Anita shrugged at him. "If Yasmin and I can tell, do you suppose Josephine can, too?"

"What will it do to her when she finds out we've been working together from the jump, that you've continued to spy on her?"

"I suppose, Zaf, that we'll burn that bridge when we come to it. Until then, you're not a captive here. Go to Dusty's, but whether you go as her bodyguard or boyfriend is to your discretion."

Zaf was neither. He was twisted-up in love with Joey, and he needed clarity more than his next breath. He wouldn't get it here at the ranch and was restless without her.

So he drove, guiding the rental pickup along June Creek's peaceful roads until he found the dive bar on Minton Street.

Joining the current of newcomers, he found people scattered. Some sat hunched over fried food, some surrounded pool and foosball tables, some occupied the bar and some were dancing on the dimly lit floor.

Joey was doing none of that. On a bar stool, her cane held between her knees and a mic in her hand, she was singing an unfamiliar country ballad while a cigarette-smoking band played on stage.

Zaf hung back, listening, falling deeper in love with every lyric she sang and the bubbles of tipsy laughter in her voice.

"What can I get you, boss?" the barkeep asked.

"Beer." He nursed the cold drink until Joey hit the final notes of her song then he slithered through the strands of folks. "Finally, that voice comes out of hiding."

Her gaze landed on him, and her smile froze when he

touched his beer to his Stetson. "You're wearing the hat? Aww, it feels like I accomplished something."

"I stand my ground on the guitar issue."

"Understood. Give and take's what it's all about."

Zaf chuckled and let her take a swig of his beer. "How drunk are you and the infamous Honey Sutherland?"

"Shots and martinis. One each. We're pathetically responsible tonight, but it's wonderful to catch up with her. We were best friends growing up. I've missed her." Joey pointed out the pretty blonde twirling and gyrating on the dance floor.

"She reminds me of how you were in Mexico," he said. "Dance with me."

"What's in this beer? You're crazy right now if you think I *can* dance."

"Just hang on." He traded the beer bottle for her cane and lifted her off the stool. In the center of the floor, he lowered her until her boots were on top of his shoes.

Joey's eyes filled. "We're dancing."

It wasn't perfect, people had to be staring and he'd never be able to give back what he'd taken from her, but this worked for them. Zaf held her around the waist and moved carefully to the slow beat, and all she had to do was trust him.

After a while she rose to her tiptoes. "I told you what'd happen if you wore the hat…"

Zaf's entire form tightened. Except, he didn't want to take more from her tonight. He wanted to give.

The end of the wraparound bar was vacant, probably because a big-ass illuminated plastic two-scoop cone advertising June Creek's own ice cream brand stood in the way.

"This cone reminds me," he told her when he brought her behind the cone. The prop's white-gold glow caressed one side of her. Partially in light, partially in shadow—that was Joey exactly. He held her still, against the bar, with a firm hand on her middle. "I haven't had dessert yet."

"I can go for a strawberry dipped."

Zaf smiled and his anticipation climbed as she ordered a cone and turned to him again when the bartender was called to the opposite end of the bar.

"I heard if you eat dessert standing up, the calories don't count," Joey said.

"What's the caloric value of this?" Zaf's fingers moved aside the fabric between her thighs and she instantly tensed up.

"Oh—not here. My friends eat at this bar."

He put the Stetson on her head, kissed the smear of strawberry ice cream on her lips. "Mmm." Off went the panties, and he stuffed them in his jeans pocket. "I'm your friend, Jo." He nudged her legs apart. "Why can't I eat at this bar, too?" He sank to his knees.

"Zaf…" was the last word to pass her lips before his lips found her. Music swam around them, the lighted prop exposed them even as it hid them, and she rocked to the rhythm of his tongue between her legs, leaving her slick and yielding for him.

"Look at me when I'm touching you."

Joey cut her moan short and it sounded more like a sharp, erotic squeak. But she watched his fingers tunnel deep and withdraw, watched his eyes as they watched her.

Returning his mouth to her mound, he drank in her taste and sucked on her flesh until she started to quake.

"Oh, there you are, Joey," someone said, and there was the sound of high heels on the plank floor.

"Oh, *God*, no," he heard Joey gasp, and she fumbled to shield herself with the hat and fight the orgasm.

But she was already coming, and a final stroke of his tongue had her crying out and crushing the ice cream cone in her fist.

And with a stunned "Whoa!" Honey Sutherland caught him going down on Joey in a bar called Dusty's.

Joey shook, her body boldly riding the sensations as she floundered to explain why Zaf was on his knees with his face between her thighs—besides the obvious truth.

"As y'all were," Honey said, snickering as she retraced her steps around the perimeter of the bar. "Welcome home."

Chapter 11

True to her word, Joey helped coordinate Danica and Dex's wedding. Within a week of her return from Texas, the Slayers' training camp had a day off, and the team's quarterback discreetly arrived at the courthouse to marry his bride in a simple late-afternoon ceremony that had brought Joey to tears.

For the first time since she'd traded princess stories for her mother's law books, she believed a relationship full of love but void of lies was a real, tangible thing.

"Thank you," Danica said to Joey, holding her bouquet out of the way so they could hug. Dex stood near the judge's chambers where the newlyweds would make a quiet exit to a waiting car. "Arranging this, being here, transforming the place. The flowers are incredible."

The floral arrangements were her gift to the couple. Though short notice, the extravagant Bonita Gardens of Texas order had arrived this morning, and a few courthouse employees Joey called friends had been happy to help put it all together.

When the room was cleared, and Joey left alone with nothing but an abundance of flowers and her thoughts, she smoothed imaginary wrinkles from her pale blue pencil dress. "It's all changing."

The lives of her friends, her relationship with everyone who loved her in Texas, her feelings toward Zaf.

There was no question that she was irretrievably in love with him. He'd told her not to love him or forgive him, but she had gone ahead and taken both actions.

Because *no one* and *nothing* controlled her heart, she realized. It functioned independently of someone else's warnings and her mind's reservations.

As with the flowers she'd nurtured growing up, she could either feed her heart what it craved, or see it wither. Take a risk or stay on the shelf.

In the parking lot Joey slid into the Ferrari but picked up her phone before turning the key.

Eddie had called. She missed the family already. He was probably following up about the autographed practice ball she'd promised him. TreShawn Dibbs had offered it to her before her trip out of town, and she had yet to pick it up to send to her football-crazed kid brother.

"*¿Bueno?*"

"*Hola, manito.* Calling you back. Is this about the football?"

"No, not that. Look, Joey, I'm just going to say this. Maybe I'm too much like Papá or it could be Mamá's right and I have a long way to go till I'm ready for the Esposito family business, but there's something you gotta know."

"What?"

"They're lying to you."

"Who? Eddie, come on—"

"Everyone's lying. Mamá and Papá know Zaf Ahmadi's the one who shot you in that messed-up bust. They know about Gian DiGorgio. Mamá put you under her protection when she hired Zaf. He's working for her."

"What?"

"Swear to God," Eddie said. "I might be a jackass for telling you, but I had to. The way you were acting with him at the reunion… I don't know, it looked like you have it bad."

Because I do and I can't hide what a fool I am.

"I had to tell you, Joey. I'm sorry."

"Shh, *está bien.*" It wasn't, though. But maybe she was too much like their mother, and found it easier to lie.

When she hung up, Joey drove home. She parked on the curb, not in the driveway beside Zaf's pickup. Next door, Aggie was in her front yard setting up sprinklers, but as Joey got out of the car, the woman trotted across the lawn.

"Joey, hey. I wanted to give you these." She pulled a small envelope from her shorts pocket. "I won a country club raffle for a pair of tickets to the erotic arts festival next month. To be honest, it's rather highbrow for me and I'm not seeing anyone. I thought you and your sexy man of mystery might go, instead. So, here."

Joey eyed the envelope. The sexy man of mystery wasn't *hers.* He'd never been. Paddling through her grief until she could form words, she said, "Thanks, Aggie."

Going directly to the guest room's walk-in closet, Joey looked around. It was a work in progress, coming together in such a way that she could see its potential. It was very much like her…

She was unfinished, messy, complicated. But she thought Zaf's patience and attention to her was a labor of friendship, if not some form of love.

It wasn't, though. The closet remodel was just a solid, a favor, a job. Being with her was the same for him.

"How was the wedding? Any paparazzi get in the way?"

When she didn't immediately answer, Zaf turned to study her through goggles. "You okay?"

"The wedding was fine."

"Good." His smile was a rare thing, and while it had the power to arrow straight to her core and make her feel laden with desire, today it only danced on her pain. "Better step back," he said, going to a sawhorse. "Don't want shavings to get all over you."

"My neighbor gave us tickets to see an erotic festival. I shouldn't have accepted them, since we're not going."

"Yeah, of course we won't go if you don't want to. Check this out. The transformation's happening. Tell your shoes they ought to have a home in another few days."

"Leave it," she whispered, but he'd begun sawing and didn't hear. "Leave it! Screw the closet."

"What the hell?"

She sobbed, but there were no tears. Going to the guest room, she almost sat on the bed before she remembered the first night they'd had sex in this house. "I know Mamá's your client. I know she's had eyes on me, even though she swore she wouldn't spy, and that she hired you."

Zaf followed close, but he didn't make the mistake of touching her. He whipped off the goggles and got in front of her. "Anita and her people are worried about you, damn it, Jo. When she presented the job, I told her no at first. I thought the best thing I could do for you was stay the hell away—"

"How right you were. What did she tell you? That I can't fend for myself? That you owed me your protection because of Arizona?"

"She said I was the best man to keep you safe."

"How much is the firm paying you? Tell me, how much am I worth to y'all?"

"Stop—"

"Oh, I want to know. And the sex? How was *that* negotiated into the deal? Are you paid bonuses for having to endure fucking me, or is that a perk for you, Zaf?"

"The sex is because you and I want it. Don't ever say it's something other than that. I can't shake you, and I've tried."

Joey shrugged. "So we have great sex. We get along that way. But it doesn't change the fact that my mother has once again interfered, and she handpicked you to guard me. It was my right to fall in love with you again on *my* terms, not because of her meddling."

Zaf froze. "You love me?"

I don't want to. I don't want to be your fool.

"I can't do this anymore, Zaf. Call my mother, tell her the job's canceled. I'm sure she won't care if you keep the money the firm paid—"

"I'm not getting money."

"What, then?"

Anguish surged in his eyes. "Anita and your uncles, they're helping me get to Pote."

Pote. Damien Pote was a drug lord who kept himself mobile and his operations fluid, and had managed to escape numerous convictions over the past fifteen years of his reign within America. He employed less influential drug-traffickers and terrorists to carry out orders.

"Was Pote involved in your cousin's murder?"

"Anita's informants say he was."

Joey hurt from head to toe. "So this was about Raphael, from the start. It's about that ring, Zaf, and this obsession you won't drop." And it dawned. "You lied to me, when you said you'd given up the hunt. You're still Archangel."

"I'm sorry."

"It's too late for apologies." She wiped her face, shook her head; everything was still havoc. "I'm going to leave for a while, give you time alone to get your things."

"Jo, don't—"
Tuning him out, Joey got in the Ferrari and drove.

Full squad practice had been especially punishing today.
Eleven hours after reporting to the main building's cafeteria for a team breakfast meeting, TreShawn felt as though someone had hacked at his muscles with a dull pickax. The media had invaded and the owners were guests at the facility. On the sidelines of the practice field, Marshall Blue and his wife had assessed each roster member and coach behind their reflective sunglasses and almighty attitudes.

Mediocrity wouldn't make the cut—not this season. Last year TreShawn had celebrated a championship win, but that didn't mean his job was secure. So today special teams had pushed hard, and he'd pushed himself harder. Ignoring the brutality of the practices and the spite spewing from short-tempered coaches as everyone reviewed the taped practices on a projector that magnified the players' every mistake, no matter how minuscule, TreShawn had battled for his job.

The Slayers performed a miracle last season and had trading leverage. To keep his name on the roster, he needed to show the special teams coordinator, the head coach, the GM and, above anyone else, the owners that when it came to the kicker position, they already had the best.

The team wasn't down to fifty-three players yet, but that would change soon after the men pissed and results came through. Teammates had talked about the coaching staff's reluctance to cut too many should they need to make adjustments for league and franchise policy violators.

But TreShawn figured that at this point, the Blues' roster was next to finalized. Some of the men sweating and bleeding through reps wouldn't step on a game field in a bloodred-and-silver uniform, and some wouldn't play a single professional game.

Anxious to protect what belonged to him, TreShawn had trudged from one end of hell to the other and back. Now he was going home—not for another stupid-ass party, but to kick back with a friend.

Minako's crossover Buick wasn't in his driveway, but a black Ferrari was.

"I was just about to leave," the driver said, getting out and coming around the back of the sweetest luxury ride he'd ever seen.

"Joey?" TreShawn could no longer remember how many times he'd invited her to his place. Each time she turned him down. She went to charity stuff, showed up at clubs, accepted invitations across the roster—but when it came to anything one-on-one, she was impossible to get. A man who wasn't sprung would've quit messing with her, but she had something more than hotness, a superb set of tits and a rockin' ass that compelled players and staff to stare.

"Hi. I stopped by for the practice ball. I should've called—"

"Hold up, hold up." He got out of his truck and met her at the rear of the car. "I like this, coming home to this. Seeing you here. You're..."

TreShawn paused, waiting for her to interrupt or twist away the way she'd been evading him the entirety of training camp.

"What am I?" she prompted in that sexy accent.

"Crying." Another step forward, and still she didn't bolt. "Where's your man?"

Joey shook her head, and he caught her jaw in his hand, settling his mouth on hers.

The exhaustion camp had left behind cracked, and adrenaline pushed through. The ghetto boy with no prospects had grown up, was getting paid big money and had a woman like this. It was the ultimate dream, and he was living it.

Pulse thundering, skin heating, he pressed close and kept her in place with a hand molding tight to her ass.

Did he taste confusion on her lips? Resistance? He wasn't certain, but she was unresponsive in his arms, until she moaned.

Wait. Or was that a sob?

"What is this?" someone shrieked behind them.

Joey pushed at him with one hand and steadied herself with her cane as he turned to see a Buick on the curb. The driver's window was down and Minako's head poked out.

"Min," he said, watching her fling herself out of the car and stomp to the other side. A car bulleted past and he almost lost his shit, but she darted safely back then threw open the passenger door.

Emerging with a wine bottle and one of those insulated bags she used whenever she brought over dinner, she deposited the items on the ground and shouted, "Take this so I don't feel like an idiot for preparing a lasagna from scratch. Go back to mauling her now."

Was she pissed? "Why are you yelling?"

"We had plans tonight."

"Chilling in front of the TV. We can do that anytime."

"No." Minako looked from him to Joey. "You're the woman from the Mirage. I thought TreShawn would leave you alone, since you have someone. But…he must be really hard up."

"Hey," he warned her, "back off. Quit sweating me, like you're my woman or something."

She drew back as if he'd hit her, and he realized he'd never wanted to see that expression on her face. Minako was fiery, tough, a scrapper—but apparently, she could be hurt.

"No, I'm not your woman, TreShawn. Just your friend. I think you'd rather have enemies than friends." She started walking, backlit by the last rays of sun melting on the horizon. Her long black hair moved through the wind like whips; the sway of her narrow but feminine hips drew his eye.

"She'll be all right." Would she? If TreShawn went to her stucco house and waited beneath her window, would she give in to a smile and come back to him?

Was he wrong to ask that of her?

"I think she's hurting," Joey said. "Coming here was an epic mistake. So was the kiss. Now two more people are casualties of the craziness that's my life. I'm leaving."

He picked up the lasagna and wine. "Wait, Joey—"

"TreShawn, I can't be what you need. And you keep looking after her car." Joey withdrew an envelope from her purse. "If you apologize and make it clear to her that I'm not in the picture, I think she'd appreciate sharing this with you."

It wasn't until after Joey fled and TreShawn sat alone in his mansion eating the meal his pissed-off friend had put together that he opened the envelope. Tickets.

An erotic festival. With Minako Sato?

Zaf was packed, keys in hand, but he'd be damned if he walked out the door without seeing Joey once more.

She loved him. What the hell was he supposed to do with that? Five years ago their hearts had been aligned, but when he'd infiltrated her world in Las Vegas he hadn't assumed—or wanted, for her sake—to reclaim the love that could bend and break them both.

Joey's family had called on him to protect her, but all he'd done was reopen the wounds he left on her heart.

In the guest bedroom, he surveyed the unfinished closet remodel. It was a simple game of geometry for him, should've been completed days ago, but so many times he'd let Joey and her busy hands and sexy talk lead him off task.

He loved her to distraction and was beyond saving.

Zaf sensed her return before he heard the front door open. Swaggering into the kitchen, following the music of her footsteps and the tap of her cane, he lingered in the entryway as she rinsed her mouth over the sink then took a handful of jelly beans from the jar.

"I saw your duffel on the couch," she said after a while. The silences between them had once been comforting. Now they hurt. "When are you leaving?"

Never, if things were different…if *they* were different. "Now. I called Anita. She wants to speak with you."

"I realize she does. I haven't answered her calls. She likely has crafted a rock-solid defense for her meddling, but I'm not in the mental state to tolerate it."

"I informed her that I'm officially off this assignment."

Joey stepped away from the counter and stopped just in front of him. Red rimmed her eyes and her chin trembled. "*Assignment?* I'm Josephine. I'm your Jo. How could you call me yours when you never wanted me?"

"I *did* want you." There it was—honesty after all was said and done, and he was on his way out the door. "I do want you."

"It's too late, Zaf. I kissed another man."

Zaf had no claim, no leverage, no room to throw his weight with her. But that didn't stop him from swearing through the initial blinding pain. "That was fast, Jo."

"Well, why waste a moment getting over you?"

It was meant to cut him off at the knees, but he returned, "You were rinsing your mouth at the sink when I came in here."

"So you're only exceptionally perceptive when it's convenient? If you were consistent, if you'd paid attention to me all this time, you would have known the moment I fell again. The last time, years passed before I let another man touch me. *Years*."

He hadn't meant to reappear in her life, resurrect her

love for him and leave her at square one. "Holding you like that wasn't my plan."

"Plans sure go awry for us, don't they?"

"Yeah, damn it, Jo. They do. I didn't *plan* to hurt you or come back and see you open up to me again. I didn't plan this. But you loving me? That's my friggin' blessing and curse." Touching her was a gift he didn't deserve, but he grabbed it, anyway. He took deliberate steps, finally cupping her shoulders. "I didn't ask for love or forgiveness."

"I gave it to you, anyway. I can't shut off my heart. I'm not like you, Archangel."

In that moment Zaf despised his code name and everything he'd done in that role. The deceit, the plotting, the killing—no matter how necessary, no matter the cause. Joey had restored his humanity and his faith that this was still a world of miracles and forgiveness and, yeah, love.

"Kissing someone else felt strange. Wrong. You push me away, say you don't want to hold me, but you keep pulling me back."

"*I'm* not pulling you back," he muttered. "This is." He brought her hand to his chest, flattened her palm over his heart. "I love you."

She untangled her hand and went to the living room to muscle his duffel bag to the floor. "You don't get to do this to me, Zaf. You can't come here on a lie and then say you love me when you're packed and ready to walk out."

He slung the duffel's strap over his shoulder.

End it here. Don't ever come back. It's over.

"Great, keep walking, Zaf."

But the note of dark grief in her voice cuffed him, holding him still. The strap slid from his shoulder, the duffel hit the floor with a thud.

Turning, he heard her breath catch before her hand knotted in his shirt and he seized her mouth. His tongue swirled in deep, and picking up the flavor of the candy and a bitter undertone of dish soap, he wanted to replace the taste with his.

"I love you, Jo," he said, unzipping her dress and peeling it off. "I didn't want this. I wanted to lie until I made it true."

"We're not easy. We're a mess."

"But good together."

"In this way." She pushed up his shirt to kiss his pecs, tongue his nipples and nuzzle his chest hair. "When we touch each other, we don't lie."

So they didn't talk. Zaf carried her and her cane to the first room he saw with a bed. He set her down and stripped her naked. She watched him, asking for nothing as he threw off his shirt and jeans.

When he joined her on the bed, she flipped to her side and he couldn't see her face. But he could feel the dampness of tears as when he brushed back her hair and his cock nudged into her from behind.

She reached back to clasp his head, and rocking with her, he said into her ear, "The love's not new. It's not something I lost and picked up again. I never stopped loving you, Josephine."

Nodding but not speaking, she tightened her hold on him and let him bring them to a point where nothing existed but the love soaking their bodies, riding on their moans and fusing them together.

Afterward Joey slipped away to the kitchen for a drink of water, and Zaf spread out over the bed, running his hand along the sheets. Her heat remained there. If he missed her when she was only on the other side of the house, how would he get by without her?

His phone rang from the pocket of his jeans, and he sprang up to get the call. The conversation was short—no salutations, just information.

It was time to go.

Zaf was pulling on his shirt when he found her perched on the counter. "How'd you manage that?"

"I functioned in this kitchen with its tall cabinets and high shelving before you came along, Zaf." Noticing that he was dressed, she asked, "You're not unpacking that duffel, are you?"

"Anita called again. A sting's being set in New Mexico—"

"Pote?"

He came to her but turned away, and her legs parted to make room for him as she kissed the back of his neck. "This is it, Joey."

"Call me Jo, until you're out the door."

"I don't think I should walk out the door. I don't want to leave you when you're still on DiGorgio's list."

Zaf felt her sigh against his skin. He was only one man—one flawed, conflicted man. He couldn't go to New Mexico and stay in Las Vegas. He couldn't avenge Raphael's death and still protect Joey.

"Go, Zaf. Finding justice for Raphael is why you wear the ring and it's the reason I was brought down. My mother's usually spot-on about these things, and if she says now is the time for you to be on the move, then listen."

"Jo…"

"Don't say it, whatever you're thinking. It'll just make this harder."

He turned around, held her gaze. "So what is this?"

"Goodbye."

Chapter 12

"I have your man."

The Slayers' random drug testing had commenced several days prior, and while three members of the squad had tested positive for marijuana—two veterans who'd rolled the dice and tried to use a masking agent that failed, and a rookie who hadn't put enough stock in the severity of the Blues' penalties for policy violation—Joey hadn't been convinced that the search was over.

Nor had she been quick to consider her job concluded when she'd heard that drug paraphernalia had turned up in TreShawn Dibbs's Vegas home.

The Blues had suspended him from team activities and prohibited him from commenting to the press and signing autographs, and the findings had been reported to the league. However, it seemed to fall into place *too* neatly and presented itself as a frame job.

Charlotte, who'd been hurt on a personal level, since her friendship with TreShawn had begun during the previous

season's camp, eventually was resigned to accept that the
man had backslid and shouldn't be granted preferential
treatment. She, along with the head coach and her parents,
had urged Joey to drop her quest to implicate someone else.

But justice was floating out there, waiting to be revealed, and she'd been unable to let it go.

Just as Zaf was unable to abandon his hunt.

From behind a colossal desk at Slayers Stadium, Marshall Blue put his hand on top of the folder Joey had placed
there. He rolled his dark eyes to his wife then authorized,
"Give us the name."

"Duncan Torsay."

"Duncan?" Tem echoed. "He's a veteran on this team."

"So were two of the players who got caught in the test,"
Joey pointed out. "Duncan offered me cocaine. He's hosting an after-testing party tomorrow night. I was invited.
According to him, his supplier will be there, providing
meth and some synthetic drugs."

"Let's get Ozzie Salvinski on the phone and have him
set up something with the authorities for this party," Marshall said, already reaching for his desk phone.

Joey cut him off, slapping her hand over the unit before
he could make contact. "Don't."

"Why not?" Tem demanded.

"Ozzie's the supplier." Mind still spinning to process
the truth, she indicated the folder. "I asked an independent
source to check up behind me. Independent source says
I'm right. My supervisor's been providing drugs to Duncan Torsay, who's been using and selling."

The following night Ozzie was arrested in a bust. Joey,
who'd refined her research skills under his tutelage at
ODC, hadn't been able to stay away from the precinct.

"Why?" she asked him.

They sat under dim whitish light, with a blank table between them. Not so long ago they'd sat at Nickel's, chatting as friends. He wasn't the man she thought he was.

Ozzie's eyes were like amber-colored stakes driving into her soul. He blamed *her*.

She tried to accept the circumstances for what they were, because so many criminals felt a compulsion to blame investigators and whistleblowers and witnesses instead of allowing themselves to be humbled with remorse.

"Why, Ozzie?"

"You're asking me that when the Blues have you driving a million-dollar car?"

"I returned the car." She had driven to the police department in her Camaro and was done trying on the Blues' ornate lifestyle. "And what you're saying is you've been selling drugs to Torsay because of the money he's offered."

"Money isn't a number in a bank account. It's power. It makes decisions."

"What kind of decisions?"

"Whether or not a man's wife sticks around or whores herself out to a guy with fatter pockets."

Joey didn't let her face reveal a reaction, but inside she cringed. Ozzie's wife had left him and set up a life with someone wealthy. "Funneling drugs to NFL players doesn't affect your ex-wife and it won't bring her back to you."

Ozzie shot out of his seat the way he had at CUT. The hair-trigger rage had been there then, and she hadn't known that to question his integrity wasn't an insult to his pride but merely something that aggravated a secret truth.

Uniforms guided him from the table, and Joey watched a man she trusted be led away. Outside the interrogation room, she waved to someone familiar.

Parker Brandt appeared unsure for the first second that their eyes met. So much attraction had crackled between them once, but that time was an unreachable memory now. He crossed the hall to her. "Hey."

"I had visitation with Ozzie Salvinski."

"I heard. How're you doing?"

"My mind's blown, but…"

"Aside from Ozzie."

Terribly. I'm in love with someone and miss him.
"Scooting along as I do."

"Try to take care of yourself, Joey. I mean that."

"Appreciate it. Listen, Parker, there's a man named Cliff who hangs out in front of CCL."

"Homeless?"

"Fairly certain. He doesn't seem keen on handouts, so I wonder if you and the gang here might watch over him for me."

Parker raised a brow. "Going someplace?"

"Thinking about it." She couldn't stand going past the guest bedroom in her house and seeing it empty. The love that lived in the place while Zaf was with her had left with him, as though he'd packed it in his duffel bag, too.

With a parting smile, Parker headed back across the hall. "Take care of yourself, Joey."

She intended to. On her own with herself to lean on, she had no other choice.

TreShawn knew who to thank for the restoral of his team privileges, but he wasn't taking his truck out on the city streets to search for Joey de la Peña.

An apology waited on his tongue and dominated his mind. Minako wasn't speaking to him—and he didn't blame her.

He was a dense SOB, but she had forgiven that.

He'd neglected her friendship, but she had forgiven that, too.

He had shown up at her old-fashioned pharmacy and confronted her with accusations that she'd used her access to pharmaceuticals to set him up for drug possession. That, she *hadn't* forgiven.

TreShawn's jersey was secure and his name cleared. Still, he was miserable. He'd spoiled himself, taking for granted the neighborhood girl with the arrogant Doberman pinscher.

Now she wouldn't answer his calls, open her balcony doors or let her dog lead her down TreShawn's street.

At the pharmacy again, the place where he'd for certain broken Minako's heart, he waited in queue at the consultation booth.

The place looked like an old-timey apothecary. Weird, but practical and charming. Like Minako.

"You don't fill your prescriptions here," she said when the folks in front of him left the counter.

"You know where I fill my scripts. You know lasagna's my favorite meal. You know how to pull me back when I'm on the verge of self-destructing."

Minako slowly looked through her plastic-framed glasses to the colleagues on the left and then on the right. Then, "Next in line!"

"Wait, Min." TreShawn hopped up onto the counter. People in queue and milling through the pharmacy's aisles began to stare.

"Please move your ass. Customers fill out forms on this counter." When he complied, she asked, "What are you trying to accomplish?"

"This is my grand gesture," he told her. "You say you're not a romantic person, but you love *Breakfast at Tiffany's* and poetry and books that have people ready to do it on the covers." He braced his arms on the counter. "Min, I watched the movie and read one of those books."

"You read a romance novel?"

"Just the sex, but yeah." At her eye roll, he sighed. "Damn, I'm messed up without you. I'm sorry I could think you'd set me up. I'm sorry for not seeing how you felt about me, or how I felt about you."

In response, Minako clamped her mouth shut and left the consultation window.

Hell. That hadn't worked. "Sorry," he said to the establishment in general, and started for the door.

"TreShawn, now *you* wait."

Minako had slipped off her white coat and was coming toward him. "First, your *grand gesture* skills suck."

"I get it, Min. I'll leave you alone."

"Second," she said, grabbing hold of his arm then hugging him around his neck as she kissed him with peach-balm-scented lips, "I'm on break and was thinking you could demonstrate the *just the sex* you've been reading lately."

It took him a solid ten seconds to trust he'd heard her correctly. But when the bell jingled over the door, and he saw her walking out, he caught her on the sidewalk, lifting her and spinning her until she laughed.

This time he wouldn't let her go.

Joey came home past midnight following Charlotte and Nate's rehearsal dinner. The wedding excitement was enough to keep her busy and *almost* distract her from the fact that once again she'd be coming home to an empty house.

Empty house, empty arms, empty heart. Zaf had taken up so much space in each, and she missed him with a yearning that'd leave her sick if she dwelled on it too long.

The man had been gone for days, but to her it felt as if a few lifetimes had passed since he'd been inside her.

It would ease, though, and she'd get on with someone new, because she was tough that way. But getting there, moment by moment, only worked if a person *wanted* it to.

She didn't want to get over Zaf. Not now that honesty

was on the table. He loved her—had always loved her. She loved him, too, yet they were apart.

"Story of my crazy life," she muttered, nosing the Camaro into the garage. She pulled her thoughts back to the flurry of maid of honor duties directly ahead. After the ceremony and reception, Charlotte and Nate would be off to the luxurious, sensual beaches of Aruba. There'd be plenty of time to contemplate her sad excuse for a love life then.

Inside she yawned all the way to the hamper that held her freshly washed pajamas, changed and started to remove her earrings as she padded with her cane to the kitchen.

At the dinner she'd had champagne, then coffee, and now needed about a pitcher of iced water.

The phone rang. Odd, as absolutely no one dialed her landline after midnight. "Hello?"

"Josephine."

"Ma—"

"Shh! Listen to me carefully, Josephine," her mother instructed, and the heavy puff of her breath on the line raised the fine hairs on Joey's skin. "Talk as if I'm one of your friends, okay? We have been tracking Gian DiGorgio's known vehicles—"

"Okay, you have to stop meddling. I'm going to hang up now. I'm tired."

"Josephine!"

"I'll call you tomorrow. *Buenas noches*—"

"He's near your home. I don't know exactly where. I've called the police—"

"You didn't." So the only thing more nerve grating than having a hovering mom was having Agent 99 as your hovering mom. Now the neighborhood could add police cruisers to the list of unusual vehicles found at Josephine de la Peña's property. She wouldn't be surprised if the neighborhood petitioned her immediate relocation.

"You're not pleased with me, I know. But, Josephine, I'm your mother first. Always."

"Sure, Mamá." She could see this leading to a drawn-out discussion and figured she'd need more water. "Hang on a sec."

Joey set the phone down and went for the pitcher.

Which she dropped to the floor when Gian DiGorgio stepped into the kitchen through the mudroom.

And *now* she was pissed.

"How the hell did you get in my house?"

"Through the garage," he said in a cavalier, mocking tone, gesturing to the mudroom. "You opened the garage and I thought it'd be easier than going through the hassle of front entry in this quiet neighborhood of yours. Please, have a seat."

Joey had looked down the barrel of a gun on numerous occasions, had been injured and struck and frightened on various levels, but never had a criminal walked freely into her home—twice.

"Leave now, Gian, and the repercussions of unlawfully entering my home might not be so severe," she said, suddenly no longer sleepy or lulled by the lingering effects of a glass of champagne. She needed total focus to talk down a crazy psychopath.

"I told you before, *belladonna*, that I could get to you anywhere. Putting that high-tech security system in place delayed me, and I'm personally offended by the inconvenience, but I can somewhat understand your need to feel protected." He glanced around. "Now the house is locked up tight, but I'm the only person inside with you. Where is he? Zafir?"

"I don't know." It was true. They hadn't made contact since he'd left. "The next time I see him, I'll tell him you popped by."

He advanced and she backed up to the counter, holding

her stick tightly. "Don't get the idea that you might strike me. I guarantee it won't benefit you."

"Gian, I'll make this perfectly simple. I'll walk you to the door, will open it and will let you walk out." She started to move, clutching the counter and the stick now.

Then his hand shot out and caught her neck.

Stunned more than physically injured—how could a living being's fingers be so cold?—she countered with a cough and dropped the cane, predicting he'd perceive her as defenseless.

Good, she thought, calm now. *I knew it would come down to you and me.*

Gian gave a full-fledged grin, but the dominance trip impacted his alertness and reflexes, and by the time he saw the glass jar in her hand, it was too late for him to change the trajectory.

The jar connected with his skull, bursting on blunt force impact and setting free dozens and dozens of jelly beans. Joey felt the skin on her hand open in several tiny spots, but the blood that began to flow like wine pouring into a goblet came from her attacker as they both crumpled to the floor.

Candy crunched under her feet, and her cane wobbled as Joey scrambled up. She groped for a phone, but realized with her breath going out in a *whoosh* that the landline receiver was sideways on the counter.

And her mother on the other end.

"Mamá!"

"*Ay, Dios mio,* are you all right?" Anita cried. "Did he hurt you? Are you okay? Where the hell are the police?"

As though on her command, sirens screamed outside on the street. "I'm okay, Mamá. The police are here. It's over. Finally, it's over, and I'm okay."

Joey supposed it made sense for her friend Charlotte to break from tradition at her wedding reception when instead of tossing her bridal bouquet from the grand second-story balcony of an elegant centuries-old ballroom, she took the staircase in measured graceful steps and joined the hundreds of guests and photographers anxious to see who'd wind up holding the bundle of rustic cream roses, branches and imported silk ribbon.

From her seat in the ballroom, Joey couldn't see much once the bride was swallowed up by single women clamoring and competing for the flowers, but with a bandaged hand she lifted her champagne flute in an early toast to the gal who'd receive them.

Charlotte appeared then, in her diamond-strapped wedding gown, holding the bouquet toward…

"Me?" Joey asked, frowning as she looked around her. Guests watched from lavishly decorated tables as lights winked up to the cherubs dancing across the stories-high ceiling.

"Yes, you," Charlotte said, handing her the bouquet. "Be happy, Joey."

"But I'm not getting married anytime soon. I don't even have a date tonight."

Around her people laughed, but did anyone—including Miz Willa Smart, who shared her table and spied her with eyes that seemed to know too much—notice the sorrow beneath her humor?

As the band struck up live classical music, Joey took the bouquet and her scepter-styled walking stick out to the gardens.

It was a beautiful summer night for a wedding…for promises and for dancing.

The lights had been magnificently webbed over the lush gardens, and the flower petals and plant leaves wore a golden blush.

"A sight like this will make me never want to leave you again."

She turned as her mouth fell into a soft O.

Zaf stepped away from the double doors and across the stone walkway to her. The music seemed to trail after him, but he had a way of amplifying everything. "Can I get a dance?"

"You came back to Las Vegas for a dance?"

Zaf drew closer and she let him kiss her: forehead, nose, lips, the bandage wrapped around her hand. "I didn't protect you, Jo."

"In a very bizarre way, you did," she protested. "The weapon I used to fend him off was a gift from you." She offered her lips again. "Why did you come back?"

"For you. I didn't go to New Mexico. I had to let Raphael rest in peace, by not hanging on to his murder." He raised a hand; his cousin's ring was gone. "I'm letting the Pote sting happen and I won't be a part of it. I came back to be with the woman I love."

He'd put her first. He loved her. It was dizzying and she didn't doubt it this time.

"Where were you if not in New Mexico?"

"A small town outside El Paso, applying for a job. There's this security firm that seems interested in my skill set."

Joey gazed at him, greedily taking in his sulky features and serious dark eyes. "The Espositos want you in the family business, do they?"

"Seems that way. I, however, want to be home with you." Holding her so that she could toe off her stilettos and settle her feet on his, he started to move to the music that caressed the gardens. "I don't know if it's here in Las Vegas."

"Or in Texas," she said truthfully. Some undefined mission, some undecipherable chapter in the arc of her life, had been completed. Underneath the bittersweet finality of it all was the certainty—as comforting as it was exhilarating—that she wasn't meant to go it alone. Not anymore.

Joey and Zaf were unfinished apart, but mesmerizingly complete together. Two halves of a whole. They were risky, intense, dirty together, and no one understood them more than each other.

"So what do you propose we do?"

That's exactly it, she thought, looking at the bouquet in her hand. *Propose.*

Zaf kissed her. "I love you, so here's what I'm hoping. Marry me, Jo."

"I will," she whispered. "I can't wait another five years for you, though. Or five months or five days. Just marry me, Zaf, and take me…"

"Somewhere for us."

There *was* such a place. They just had to search for it. For now, they had a diamond sky, a golden garden and this dance.

* * * * *

SPECIAL EXCERPT FROM

Elite boutique owner Autumn Dupree is a realist when it comes to relationships. Until nightclub owner Ajay Reed arouses a passion she never knew existed...

Read on for a sneak peek at FALLING FOR AUTUMN, the next exciting installment of Sherelle Green's BARE SOPHISTICATION series!

"What am I going to do about this?" she said aloud to the empty alley.

"For starters, how about you avoid walking out into dark alleys by yourself."

Her head flew to the door she had just exited and her eyes collided with his. No man had a right to look that sexy. Ajay had on a black shirt and dark jeans. But instead of his usual footwear, he had on a pair of black shoes. The lines of his fade and goatee were so clean, there was no doubt that he'd just gotten a haircut. He took a few steps closer to her until he was standing under the same light she was.

"Why did you come out here?"

"I needed to breathe."

He studied her eyes, and it took all her energy to stand there and not fidget under his intense gaze. Her breathing was scattered and her heart felt as if it had actually skipped a beat.

"Why were you flirting with Luke? I thought you didn't like him like that."

"I don't. But…" Her voice trailed off when she realized she had been about to tell him the truth.

"But what?"

She couldn't believe she was really contemplating telling him. "He told me that the longer he hugged me, the more upset you would get."

"He said that?"

"Yes. He also told me that the minute he kissed my cheek, the vein in your neck would pop. Then he told me to see what would happen if I placed my arm on his shoulder."

He squinted in curiosity. "So, were you trying to get a rise out of me to please him…or yourself?"

She swallowed the lump in her throat as her gaze bounced from his eyes to his lips. "I think it was a little bit of both. It was his birthday, so I was being polite. But I also wanted to see how you would react."

His eyes dropped to her lips. "You don't want to play games with a man like me, Autumn."

Don't miss
FALLING FOR AUTUMN by Sherelle Green,
available April 2016 wherever
Harlequin® Kimani Romance™
books and ebooks are sold!

REQUEST YOUR FREE BOOKS!

2 FREE NOVELS
PLUS 2 FREE GIFTS!

KIMANI™
ROMANCE

Love's ultimate destination!

YES! Please send me 2 FREE Harlequin® Kimani™ Romance novels and my 2 FREE gifts (gifts are worth about $10). After receiving them, if I don't wish to receive any more books, I can return the shipping statement marked "cancel." If I don't cancel, I will receive 4 brand-new novels every month and be billed just $5.44 per book in the U.S. or $5.99 per book in Canada. That's a savings of at least 16% off the cover price. It's quite a bargain! Shipping and handling is just 50¢ per book in the U.S. and 75¢ per book in Canada.* I understand that accepting the 2 free books and gifts places me under no obligation to buy anything. I can always return a shipment and cancel at any time. Even if I never buy another book, the two free books and gifts are mine to keep forever.

168/368 XDN GH4P

Name	(PLEASE PRINT)	
Address		Apt. #
City	State/Prov.	Zip/Postal Code

Signature (if under 18, a parent or guardian must sign)

Mail to the **Reader Service**:
IN U.S.A.: P.O. Box 1867, Buffalo, NY 14240-1867
IN CANADA: P.O. Box 609, Fort Erie, Ontario L2A 5X3

Want to try two free books from another line?
Call 1-800-873-8635 or visit www.ReaderService.com.

* Terms and prices subject to change without notice. Prices do not include applicable taxes. Sales tax applicable in N.Y. Canadian residents will be charged applicable taxes. Offer not valid in Quebec. This offer is limited to one order per household. Not valid for current subscribers to Harlequin® Kimani™ Romance books. All orders subject to credit approval. Credit or debit balances in a customer's account(s) may be offset by any other outstanding balance owed by or to the customer. Please allow 4 to 6 weeks for delivery. Offer available while quantities last.

Your Privacy—The Reader Service is committed to protecting your privacy. Our Privacy Policy is available online at www.ReaderService.com or upon request from the Reader Service.

We make a portion of our mailing list available to reputable third parties that offer products we believe may interest you. If you prefer that we not exchange your name with third parties, or if you wish to clarify or modify your communication preferences, please visit us at www.ReaderService.com/consumerschoice or write to us at Reader Service Preference Service, P.O. Box 9062, Buffalo, NY 14240-9062. Include your complete name and address.

KROM15

Turn your love of reading into rewards you'll love with
Harlequin My Rewards

**Join for FREE today at
www.HarlequinMyRewards.com**

Earn **FREE BOOKS** of your choice.

Experience **EXCLUSIVE OFFERS** and contests.

Enjoy **BOOK RECOMMENDATIONS**
selected just for you.

PLUS! Sign up now
and get **500** points
right away!

Earn **FREE** REWARDS
HarlequinMyRewards.com
Join Today!

*They're discovering
the healing powers
of passion…*

POSSESSED
BY PASSION

NEW YORK TIMES BESTSELLING AUTHOR

POSSESSED BY PASSION

Architect Hunter McKay came home to Phoenix to open
her own firm, not rekindle her romance with Tyson Steele.
But when she runs into the playboy, Hunter fears she's
headed straight for heartbreak once again. Still, Tyson hasn't
forgotten the one who got away. Can he convince this sensual
woman that he's the real deal—that they deserve a second
chance together?

FORGED OF STEELE

Available March 2016!

"This deliciously sensual romance ramps up the emotional stakes
and the action with a bit of deception and corporate espionage.
Short, sexy, and sizzling." —*Library Journal* on *Intimate Seduction*

HARLEQUIN®
www.Harlequin.com

KPBJ410316